Wards of the Women introduces three desperate girlfriends who, on the surface, appear to have it all, but underneath are in the midst of various crises. Mysterious deaths, extortion, straying husbands and illegitimate children have suddenly overtaken the lives of Violet Christianson, Shayne Wentworth, and Fifi Gentry. Eventually, when Violet becomes fed up with all of their circumstances, she does what any sensible woman would do—blackmails the state prison warden into letting each of them buy an inmate from the jail for their own personal fulfillment. But never in their wildest dreams did they imagine all the chaos that would ensue from a simple little purchase.

Wards of the Women
Copyright © 2019 Denise N. Wheatley
ISBN: 978-1-4874-2546-3
Cover art by Martine Jardin

Published by eXtasy Books Inc or
Devine Destinies, an imprint of eXtasy Books Inc

Look for us online at:
www.eXtasybooks.com or www.devinedestinies.com

# Wards of the Women

## By

## Denise N. Wheatley

# DEDICATION

*To my mother Donna, for being my everything . . .*

"A woman is like a tea bag—you never know how strong she is until she gets in hot water."
~Eleanor Roosevelt

# THE PRETENSE

# CHAPTER ONE

Violet Christianson was a woman who knew what her name meant to most. *Perfection*. Everyone either wanted her, wanted to be her, or simply wanted her to go away.

Violet considered herself to be the most beautiful woman on her block and never missed an opportunity to ponder her stunning image. At five-eight, she kept her lean size two figure draped in outrageously expensive designer clothing at all times. Her dazzling, widespread hazel eyes were framed with long, lush lashes. Her retroussé nose had finally been perfected after several invasive surgeries. Her soft, plump lips accentuated high cheekbones when they puckered. Her raven hair swung so low that she could practically sit on it.

Violet's husband, Elliot, was rich. The richest man on the block, to be exact. Elliot worked as a real estate developer and closed more big-money deals than most. As a result, he allowed her to spend his money on whatever she wanted, and whenever she wanted. As he should have, considering how unsightly he was. Elliot's pockmarked skin, hair plugs, bifocaled eyes, rat-like teeth, pot belly, and squat body were enough to send most into hysterics the moment they laid eyes on him. But Elliot was wise enough to hide his ghastly appearance behind his vast fortune. So by the time people noticed his looks, they'd already been so blinded by his *Benjamins* that his ugliness became a blur. Which was exactly how he said he wanted it.

Violet's house was big. The biggest house on her suburban block, to be exact. It boasted a huge great room, six bedrooms, eight bathrooms, an Olympic-size pool, and even a room designated just for gift wrapping. The house had been designed by Jacques Lolique, interior decorator to the stars, which meant that her contemporary décor was nothing short of flawless—as was the house's appearance, which was constantly being serviced by a small army of workers.

To top it all off, Violet was smart. Smart enough to have earned a doctorate in psychology. But rather than open a high-end practice and service the rich and famous, she'd gone with her heart and decided to work with inmates at the local state prison.

Violet Christianson. Beautiful, lucky, *and* charitable. All the reasons why most people either wanted her, wanted to be her, or simply wanted her to go away.

# CHAPTER TWO

Shayne Wentworth loved how the mere mention of her name brought smiles to most faces. She knew she might not have been the most beautiful woman on the block, but she certainly was the sweetest.

Shayne was an ex-pageant queen. Ex, simply because she now had five beautiful children and a wonderful husband to look after. If it weren't for them, she could certainly still be competing. Because, after all, when she looked at herself, her bright-green eyes still danced. She made sure her straight white teeth still gleamed. And her creamy, clear skin still glowed. As for her shoulder-length platinum blonde locks, all she'd have to do was pull them out of the bun that she usually wore and shake it out a bit. As for her figure, all it would take was a crunch or two to get back in fighting shape. And as for the rest? Nothing a tube of lip gloss and a dazzling evening gown couldn't fix. So, all things considered, she was still a contender.

Shayne's husband might not have been the richest man on the block, but he certainly was the most powerful. Russell worked as a criminal defense attorney and had a reputation for being ruthless and cutthroat. At home, however, he was a different man. Russell was a gentle pussycat who worshipped his wife and doted on his children. He allowed Shayne to stay at home while he worked to provide for the family. Which was good for her, considering she knew nothing beyond the world of pageantry.

Shayne might not have had the biggest house on the block, but the one she did have was bursting with energy. Her sixteen-year-old son, Matthew, was following in his father's star-studded footsteps by playing football at Russell's high school alma mater. Her fourteen-year-old daughter, Sloane, was a straight-A student who'd managed to skip two grades and was taking accelerated courses in high school. Her twelve-year-old son, Ryan, already knew he wanted to be an attorney, so he spent every possible moment with his dad at the law firm. Eleven-year-old Cadence was carrying her mother's torch by competing in statewide beauty pageants and winning numerous trophies and prizes. And Basil, Shayne's ten-year-old son, was simply brilliant. His wit, intellect, and cunning sense of humor amazed all who knew him.

Shayne Wentworth. Nurturing, fortunate, and fulfilled. She might not have had the best on the block, but at least she had her family.

# CHAPTER THREE

Fifi Gentry knew that the mere mention of her name meant only one thing to most. Business. And while she might not have been the sweetest woman on the block, she certainly was the feistiest.

Fifi was a go-getter. A five-foot dynamo. A twenty-eight-year-old spitfire who was too busy fighting for the rights of others to worry about trivial things. Like looks, for instance. Fifi would much rather spend her time amending proposals than getting a makeover. She did, however, put forth an effort to appear presentable, considering she wanted to be taken seriously.

Fifi never missed her monthly hair appointments to have her sleek brown bob, which complemented her almond-shaped eyes, dyed and trimmed. She cleansed her flawless olive skin with plain water and smoothed *Vaseline* over it every night, which was her secret to keeping it radiant. She followed a strict macrobiotic diet and practiced *Ashtanga* yoga to help keep her enviable size zero in shape. And she did take the time to lengthen her lashes with mascara, brighten her cheeks with blush, and accentuate her lips with gloss every day.

Fifi might have been the only woman on the block without a husband, but her boyfriend certainly was the most influential man in the state. Senator Edward Hynes was Fifi's current beau, and the buzz amongst politicians was that he'd be the one to beat during the next presidential election. And even though Fifi and Edward didn't share many of the same political views, she couldn't have been prouder of him.

Fifi's house might not have been bursting with energy, but at least it was all hers. She still lived in the home she'd grown up in, which her parents had been kind enough to give to her. She hadn't changed much by way of décor because she loved having the feel of her parents and memories of her childhood surrounding her. And the house would be perfect for raising a family in, which she was definitely looking forward to doing one day.

Fifi might not have the goods to compete in beauty pageants, but her advocacy work more than made up for that. Fifi worked as a lobbyist assistant, fighting to have bills passed that would enforce tougher child protection laws. She was currently lobbying to have convicted child molesters serve harsh, mandatory jail sentences, then once they were released, have electronic tracking devices implanted inside their bodies so their whereabouts could be traced at all times. More importantly, she was working to have a bill passed that would force child molesters to undergo physical castration.

Fifi Gentry. Purposeful, altruistic, and unrelenting. She might not have had the most on the block, but at least she had a mission.

# THE TRUTH

# CHAPTER FOUR

Violet Christianson was indeed beautiful. Due in part to her skilled plastic surgeon. After all, at the age of forty-two, Violet's wrinkle-free skin and taut abs weren't being maintained by nature alone—which was where standing appointments with Dr. Friedman came into play. That size two body? A combination of lipo, cigarettes, and starvation. Those dazzling, widespread hazel eyes? Accentuating contacts and *Botox*. Those lush lashes? Individually applied extensions. That retroussé nose? A look that had taken three surgeries to achieve. Those lips? Collagen. That hair? Extensions.

Violet's husband was indeed rich. He was also dead. The stress of having to close all those big-money deals, along with his endless consumption of donuts, fried chicken, ice cream, et cetera, eventually brought on diabetes. Which eventually sent him into a diabetic coma. Which eventually killed him. So no longer did Violet have to ask to spend all the money that Elliot always allowed her to spend anyway. Because it, along with his business, was all hers now. As it should have been, considering all that he'd put her through.

To others, Violet did appear to have it all. But the one thing that was missing in her life was children. She had dreamed of having children ever since she had been a child. And when she'd married Elliot fifteen years ago, she'd immediately begun working to make that dream a reality.

But that reality had taken a little longer than she'd expected. So long, that by the time she'd finally gotten pregnant, Elliot had decided he no longer wanted children. He'd told her he'd come too far in his career to be interrupted by something as time-consuming as a child. He was just too busy closing deals. Too ambitious trying to close more. And most importantly, too uninterested to even be bothered.

When she'd heard those words come out of her husband's mouth, Violet had become violent. She'd stormed into their library and began crashing Dale Chihuly glass sculptures into the shiny hardwood floors. She'd torn antique, limited-edition books from the shelves and ripped them into pieces. She'd grabbed the sterling silver candelabra that Elliot's mother had given them for their first wedding anniversary, wound her arm, and prepared to pitch it through the glass picture window. That was when Elliot had snatched the candelabra from her and in one swift motion, slammed the bottom of it into her stomach.

And that was it. Violet had miscarried her baby and had never been able to conceive again. That was why years later, one could understand her rage when she'd found out that Elliot had impregnated Madison, his business partner's daughter. Violet had expected Madison to have an abortion. She'd been stunned when Madison had decided to have the baby. And absolutely floored when Elliot had agreed to be a part of the child's life in an attempt to keep those big-money deals closing amicably with his business partner. It was quite unfortunate that Elliot had died shortly before Madison was due to give birth.

As for Violet's job counseling prison inmates? It wasn't just for charity. It was a way of healing herself, because Violet's father had been mentally ill. Not just *eccentric* as her family liked to call him, but an extreme schizophrenic. However, mental illness had always been considered taboo in his circles. So her father had gone untreated. Which meant he was not in his right mind when he'd stormed into a Catholic church service one evening with a gun in hand and accused the priest of molesting him throughout his childhood. Which ludicrous, considering her father grew up a devout Jehovah

Witness and had never stepped foot inside a Catholic church. Fortunately for him, when he'd shot the priest, it hadn't been fatal.

Despite Violet's father's mental state, he was sentenced to twenty-five years in a maximum-security prison. His lawyer appealed and had him reevaluated, insisting that he belonged in a mental hospital. But his appeal was denied, and after spending less than a year in prison, Violet's father had hung himself.

And so came the start of Violet's crusade to help inmates receive the proper counseling, medication, and transfers to mental hospitals when necessary. In turn, her work became the therapy she needed in order to help cope with her father's tragic death. Unfortunately, Violet had to retire after her husband's death, because she just couldn't deal with the stress of it all.

Violet Christianson. Nipped, tucked, and severely damaged. All the reasons why most people really wouldn't want her, want to be her, or even care whether or not she went away. But lucky for her, none of them knew the truth.

# CHAPTER FIVE

Shayne Wentworth was indeed an ex-pageant queen. But not the type of pageant queen one might expect. As a matter of fact, she never really competed in pageants. They were more like contests. Contests — meaning wet t-shirt, best gams, best tush, et cetera.

As for her green eyes? They only danced when they were focused on her old *pageantry* footage. Those straight white teeth? They only gleamed after they'd been bleached, which she hadn't had done in years. That creamy, clear skin? It only glowed after sex, which she hadn't had in over two years. Those platinum blonde locks? If she were to pull them out of that bun, she'd unleash a mass of over-processed frizz. As for her figure? Shayne had blown up to two hundred and fifteen pounds in recent years, so it would actually take way more than a crunch or two to get back in fighting shape.

Shayne's husband, Russell, was indeed the most powerful man on the block. But at home, he wasn't as gentle, worshipping, or doting as one might think. The only reason Shayne was allowed to stay home was because the working goals she'd set for herself were simply too unrealistic. Her dream of parlaying her *pageantry* career into modeling on the catwalks of New York and Paris never died. But at five-foot-four and armed with a double chin, blubbery belly, wide hips, celluloid-infested thighs, and rather short legs, her hope was fading fast. Especially now that she'd just turned thirty-seven.

But the main reason why Russell wasn't necessarily gentle, worshipping, and doting toward his wife and children was because he no longer lived with them. He had left his family for a number of reasons, the main one being the growing repulsion he'd developed for his wife.

Shayne had met Russell sixteen years ago at a *Best Breasts In Show* contest that she'd competed in—and won. When he'd seen her bounce onto the stage to accept her twenty-five-dollar cash prize, he knew she was the woman he'd spend the rest of his night with. Russell later told Shayne that he was determined to bed her, who he'd deemed a drop-dead gorgeous sex kitten. And he did. Over and over and over again, until she got pregnant the following year. By that time, he said he was so in love with her body that he figured he'd eventually fall in love with her mind and decided to propose. She eagerly accepted, and they'd been married with child after child ever since.

Once their youngest son was born, Russell insisted that Shayne get her tubes tied. She did, and so began the start of her incessant eating. It was as if she had lost something by not being able to get pregnant again and attempted to fill the void with food. That was how she'd inflated to two hundred and fifteen pounds.

Eventually, Russell told Shayne that when he looked at her, Fat Bastard from *Austin Powers* came to mind. He found her absolutely revolting. Her bloated face, droopy breasts, flabby arms, and doughboy stomach were more than he could handle. But there were other things about her he found repugnant as well. Like the way she smacked her lips and flashed the food in her mouth when she ate—especially tuna salad. And the way she belched and passed gas whenever and wherever they were—even in crowded elevators. And the way the belches smelled of rotten salami and the gas smelled of steamy horse dung. And the way her lips always looked so wet with pungent saliva—especially when she wanted to kiss him hello or goodbye. And the way she rubbed her fleshy body up against his in an attempt to initiate sex.

But Russell also told her that being an offensive wife wasn't the only reason he'd left home. He also left because of their children. Their overbearing, embarrassing, and crazy children. Shayne and Russell's oldest son, Matthew, was indeed a football player. The problem was, he sucked. The only reason the coach had even let him on the team was because he'd hoped Matthew would live up to his father's legacy. No such luck. But when Matthew got kicked off the team, Russell told Shayne it wasn't because their son was such a horrible player. It was because the coach had found out Matthew was gay and had seduced the star quarterback.

The couple's daughter, Sloane, was indeed a straight-A student who'd skipped two grades. But, unfortunately, that big jump gave her early access to high school boys. Senior class, high school boys to be exact—which explained how she'd met and let the senior class president talk her into cutting class and going to the movies one Monday afternoon. It was there that Sloane was caught with her head in the president's lap. When the theater manager flashed his light on them and asked for an explanation, the senior was too busy convulsing, and Sloane was too busy choking to give him a decent answer.

As for Ryan, the twelve-year-old aspiring lawyer, Russell couldn't pay him to stay away from his law office. And he was willing to give him any amount of money to do so. Because when Ryan was there, he created a total ruckus. Russell's colleagues felt obligated to give Ryan work to do, but no matter the task, he always managed to muck it up. Like when he'd tried to alphabetize a few file folders. It had taken Russell's assistant days to figure out what Ryan had done, considering he'd rearranged every file in the office. Or the time he'd re-shelved the books in the law library in a way that no one could understand. Or when he'd distributed the company's mail and failed to match any of the names on the envelopes with the names on the inboxes. All this, along with his failing grades, prompted Shayne to take Ryan to see several specialists. By the time they found out he had dyslexia, Russell informed Shayne that he no longer cared. He'd chalked his son's problem up to just being slow a long time ago.

Cadence, the miniature beauty queen, certainly did win most of her pageants. According to the inscriptions on her endless number of trophies and ribbons, she was the prettiest, most talented, most poised, et cetera. But Cadence's competition was tough. Pageant girls were fierce. So fierce that Cadence worked rigorously to maintain her winning status. A low-fat diet, daily runs on the treadmill, regular hair appointments, facials, manis, and pedis were a must.

While Russell admired his daughter's drive, Shayne envied it. If only she had the energy to follow such a strict regimen, she could start competing again and give her daughter a run for her money. But she didn't, which was so frustrating, especially when Russell chastised Shayne for allowing her child to be more motivated and disciplined than she was.

But Russell seemed to have changed his tune the evening he went to Cadence's bedroom to kiss her goodnight. He had told Shayne that when he realized she wasn't there, he went to the bathroom, where he heard her throwing up on the other side of the door. He tried to open it, but the door was locked. He called her name, but she couldn't hear him over the running water. So Russell stood there and waited for her to come out. But when she shut the water off, he listened to her laugh into the telephone and tell her best friend that she'd just stuck her finger down her throat for the fourth time that day. She insisted that three times was usually her limit, but after eating three plain M&Ms after dinner, a fourth was totally necessary. Russell just shook his head and slumped back downstairs to fix himself a drink and glowered at Shayne as he complained.

And then there was Basil. The witty genius. The charming

intellectual. *The one to watch* as everyone referred to him. Little did they know that he was really a raging bully who had beaten up practically every kid in the neighborhood. At the tender age of ten, he had already been transferred to three different schools. He'd been caught smoking his grandfather's cigars on more than a few occasions. Shayne and Russell had found several dead squirrels in the backyard that Basil had struck with his self-made bow and arrow. And when cognac had gone missing from his study, Russell had immediately gone into Basil's bedroom while he was sleeping, put his nose to his mouth, and waited for him to exhale. When he did, out came the faint scent of Kelt. That was when Russell packed his bags and walked out on what he called his delusional wife and troubled brood.

Shayne Wentworth. Unappealing, abandoned, and no longer a pageant contender. All the reasons why most people would understand that underneath it all, she wasn't nearly as sweet as she once was. Lucky for her, they had yet to look that deep.

# CHAPTER SIX

Fifi Gentry was definitely a go-getting advocate who was more concerned with her cause than her looks. Which was a good thing, considering she wasn't working with much by way of looks anyway.

That sleek brown bob of hers? Stringy was actually a more accurate way to describe it. Even the layers that Fifi had cut into it each month didn't help, considering there was no chance of it ever thickening her limp locks. Those almond-shaped eyes of hers? Crooked and close-set was more like it. Fifi's eyes only appeared almond-shaped to those who had trouble seeing. Her olive skin was definitely flawless, but it was her unplanned pregnancy, not *Vaseline*, that was responsible for its radiance. As for her size zero frame? Fifi was certainly tiny, but her body was nothing short of slight and boyish and usually went unnoticed underneath her drab tees, grungy jeans, and shabby sneakers. As for the makeup she took the time to apply every day? It was pretty much a waste, considering no amount of mascara could lengthen her spare lashes, no amount of blush could flush her gaunt cheekbones, and no amount of gloss could plump her nonexistent lips.

Fifi was indeed involved with the most influential man in the state. But he wasn't her boyfriend. He wasn't anyone's boyfriend. He was somebody's husband. But not Fifi's—which made the fact that she was pregnant with his child all the more complicated.

Fifi had met Senator Edward Hynes a little over a year ago at an anti-abortion rally. He was there giving a speech in a show of his support. She was there demonstrating and causing a ruckus. Fifi yelled, screamed, and swung her sign throughout the senator's entire speech. By the time the rally was over, her voice was so hoarse that she could barely speak. Which was why she couldn't protest when he pulled her around to the back of the stage where no one could see them. Fifi feared for her life. But the senator didn't want to kill her. He wanted to compliment her on how passionate she was about her cause. Then he bent down and kissed her. And asked if he could take her to dinner the next night. Fifi was flabbergasted. Things like that never happened to her. Plus, she hadn't been out on a date in years. So she agreed to go.

Fifi should have known better. But she didn't. She'd only researched the senator's political views, not his personal life. Which was why she'd allowed that one dinner to catapult them into an all-out love affair. But even when she did find out about the senator's marriage, Fifi went into denial and refused to leave him. She tried to ignore the glances and whispers coming from her family and friends. But she couldn't. She wished she hadn't fallen in love with him. But she had. And when she found out that she was pregnant with his baby, Fifi wished she wasn't happy. But she was.

Senator Hynes, on the other hand, was not. He'd made it clear that he would never leave his wife when Fifi confronted him about her. But she didn't listen. He'd never considered his and Fifi's occasional romps in the sack an all-out affair. But she had. He could've sworn she'd told him that she was on the pill. But she hadn't. And now, in spite of his strong anti-abortion stance, he'd begun making threats and insisting that she terminate the pregnancy. But she wouldn't. Which wasn't good for Edward—because having a baby outside of his marriage would be the death of his run for the presidency. Which he was determined to accomplish. *By any means necessary*.

Fifi might have still been living in the house that she'd grown up in, but it wasn't because her parents had given it to her. It was because they'd left it to her now that they were dead. They'd been found lying in the bedroom of their Malibu summer home a few months before, burnt to a crisp. The fire chief said that the blaze had probably been caused by an electrical problem. But some of the neighbors had witnessed the house burst into flames, as if there'd been some sort of explosion. Fifi was convinced that if there had indeed been an explosion, it was a result of the electrical problem. But her family and friends weren't buying it. They all believed that Senator Hynes had caused the fire in order to send her a message.

Fifi Gentry. Pregnant, in denial, and possibly in danger. All the reasons why most people now considered her the dumbest rather than the feistiest woman on the block. Lucky for her, that was exactly what she wanted.

# THE DISCUSSION

# CHAPTER SEVEN

"Rita?" Violet called out over the intercom. "Another round, please!"

Seconds later Rita came scurrying into the sunroom where Violet was sitting across from Shayne and Fifi.

"Thanks, sweetie," Shayne said after Rita poured more hot chocolate into her cup, then plunked three sugar cubes into the already sweetened drink and topped it off with a mountain of whipped cream and three maraschino cherries, just the way she liked it.

Fifi shook her head at Shayne as Rita filled her cup with decaffeinated green tea.

"Sugar, Miss?" Rita asked.

"Now you know better." Fifi smiled. She took a sip of the bitter drink. "Mmm, good. Thank you."

Rita shuffled over to Violet and bent down to pour more Bailey's and coffee into her cup. "Hold the coffee this time," Violet requested, lighting a cigarette and watching as Shayne obliviously chomped on her second double chocolate donut while Fifi delightfully popped a dried apricot into her mouth. Neither of them would look her way. Their avoidance was becoming quite irritating.

"So," Violet began after Rita left the room. "Are we done with all the small talk?"

Fifi swirled her tea around in her cup while Shayne licked the frosting from her hand, both acting as if they hadn't heard a thing.

"Wow. What friends," Violet scoffed, flicking ashes into a crystal tray.

"What?" Fifi responded. "We are friends!"

"*Good* friends," Shayne added with hurt in her voice.

20

Violet took a long sip from her cup, then sighed deeply. "Why is it that each of us knows what's going on with the other, but we're too afraid to discuss it?"

"Because . . ." Fifi began before her voice trailed off. She twirled a limp lock of hair around her middle finger and seemed to search for the right thing to say. "Well . . . if we already know what's going on with one another, then there's no need to discuss anything."

Shayne finished off her donut, then began ogling a vanilla long john with pink sprinkles on top.

"*Shayne*," Violet snapped. "Will you stop obsessing over the pastries and say something?"

"Huh?" Shayne huffed innocently while still staring down at the long john. "I've been talking ever since I got here."

"Yeah, but about what?" Violet asked, throwing her hands up in frustration. "Window treatments? Miss Universe? The weekend box office? Who gives a shit? We've got more important things to discuss."

"I don't wanna talk about it." Fifi rubbed her slightly bulging belly. "I'm tired, I'm nauseous, and I'm fat."

"You won't be complaining once those ta-tas start filling out." Violet smirked, laying her head back and blowing smoke rings up toward the ceiling.

"I've never wanted big breasts," Fifi replied as she pursed her lips and eyed Violet's sizable silicone mounds.

"Big breasts are beautiful." Shayne leaned forward and quickly snatched up the long john, shoving half of it inside her mouth. "I used to make a lot of money off of mine. Helped me get a husband, too."

"My sentiments exactly," Fifi murmured under her breath.

"Rita!" Violet chirped into the intercom after watching crumbs fly from Shayne's mouth. "We need the vacuum cleaner in here."

When Rita hustled into the room with the *Hoover*, Violet

pointed down at Shayne's feet. Then she looked from Fifi to Shayne shamefully.

"Well, then. I guess I have no choice but to start this dreaded conversation myself, since the two of you are being so ridiculous. Now, Elliot's bastard child is going to be born soon, and the bitch who's having it has been calling me insisting that I pay her child support. My lawyer's all over it. But in the meantime, the bitch's father is hoarding money that's owed to me from the deals Elliot closed before he died, plus he's trying to steal Elliot's half of the business."

Violet paused, placing her cigarette between her lips and inhaling deeply in an attempt to control her trembling voice. After several moments, she continued.

"But the thing that hurts the most is that my husband managed to bless some slut with a child, knowing that was the one thing I wanted more than anything else."

"*Why?*" Shayne asked right before she finished off her donut.

"I'm sorry, sweetie," Fifi said to Violet, looking guilty covering her pregnant belly.

"Vi, motherhood is overrated." Shayne rolled her eyes and licked her fingers. "Take my word for it." She stared over at the pastry tray and reached for another donut, then quickly withdrew her hand. "I've got to stop. See, this is why I'm alone now."

"You wouldn't be alone if you'd take my advice and go see Dr. Friedman. Let him fix you up a bit," Violet told her.

"All that's not necessary," Fifi said. "All you need to do is let me put together a healthy, organic menu plan for you, start a beginners yoga—"

"No, no, *no!* I don't wanna be put to sleep and sliced all up, nor do I want to eat leaves and berries and distort my body on some sweaty mat for two hours, thank you both very much. And I could have sworn my vows said 'til death do us part, not 'til fat do us part."

Shayne grabbed an apple fritter and shoved it inside her mouth, then closed her eyes and chewed slowly.

Fifi shook her head and cringed. "Here, why don't you try some of these?" She picked up a bowl of dried fruit and tried to hand it to Shayne.

"Get that away from me! It looks like rotten potpourri."

"Shayne, I know you're having problems with your children, but what's your issue with motherhood overall?" Violet asked.

"Once you have children, you cease to exist. Your only point of living is to take care of them. Plus, if I can be totally honest here, I never really wanted kids. All I wanted was to be a jet-setting top model. But then I met Russell, fell in love, and had children because I thought that would make him happy. And what'd he do? Up and leave me to raise them by myself. And to add insult to injury, do you all know he told me that I'm the reason he's turned asexual?"

"Wait, *what*?"

"Russell said I've turned him asexual!"

Violet closed her eyes and held up her hand. "Now I've heard of a man suddenly discovering he's gay, or into bestiality, or even necrophilia. But asexuality?"

"Exactly!" Shayne turned from Violet to Fifi with wide eyes. "Can you believe that? Russell is actually claiming that I've turned him off of human beings altogether. He said that after hearing all the hideous sounds my body makes and smelling all the sickening odors I emit . . . he never wants to have physical contact with another person ever again."

"That is so cruel," Fifi told her before staring down at the floor. "But I guess it's no worse than what's been said to me."

Shayne smacked her lips sympathetically. "I know. You still don't believe that Edward had anything to do with your parents being—"

"What is he saying about the baby now?" Violet asked in an attempt to shut Shayne up.

"That he still doesn't want it. And that if I'm as smart as he knows I am, I'll abort it . . . or else."

Shayne's mouth fell open. "So after doing what he did to you and your family, he's *still* threatening you?"

"What do you mean?" Fifi asked. "What did he do?"

"He had your parents—"

"Can I have Rita get you all anything else?" Violet asked, throwing Shayne a look.

She ignored her glaring stare and looked down at her watch. "It's lunchtime, isn't it?"

"I'm not hungry," Fifi said before pointing at Shayne. "So you still believe that Edward had my parents killed?"

Shayne's focus remained glued to her watch. She silently twisted it around her wrist. Violet raised her eyebrows indifferently and lit a third cigarette.

"I already told you he had nothing to do with it," Fifi said. "The fire chief confirmed that."

"Officials have been known to lie under certain circumstances," Shayne replied indignantly before finally looking up at her.

Fifi turned to Violet, obviously waiting for her to say something. When she didn't, Fifi slammed her glass down. "Vi, weren't you the one who started this conversation off with *wow, what friends*? Well, I guess you were right!"

"Fifi, you know we're your friends. That's why we're being honest with you."

"Oh, you wanna get honest?" Fifi squealed, leaning forward and cocking her head to the side. "Okay, then, let's get honest. Violet, I honestly think that you've worn out your welcome at Dr. Friedman's office. Because these days, the only thing that seems to move on your face is your bottom lip. And Shayne? I honestly think that your horrible children are bringing down the neighborhood. As a matter of fact, the thought of raising my child across the street from them is quite disturbing."

Violet choked on cigarette smoke. Shayne dropped her porcelain cup. Luckily it was empty and didn't stain the carpet. Fifi crossed her arms and glared at them both.

"Excuse me, Miss," Rita said, interrupting the showdown. "It's almost lunchtime. What would you like for me to—"

"Not now." Violet held her hand up without taking her gaze off of Fifi. Shayne watched longingly as Rita slinked out of the room, looking as though she wished she could make a request. Then she seemed to remember the situation at hand and turned her attention back to her friends.

"What the hell is your problem?" she asked Fifi.

"I don't have a problem."

"Look, we're here to support one another, not tear each other down. But how can we do that if we're not honest with ourselves first, let alone each other? Beyond that, it's time to put our heads together and figure out how to get ourselves out of these situations that we're in. We've wallowed and cried behind closed doors for long enough. Now let's stop attacking one another and brainstorm on where we should go from here."

"Can we do it over lunch?" Shayne asked, her stomach growling loudly despite all the pastries she'd eaten.

"Fine," Violet said before hitting the intercom button. "Rita!"

"Well, I'm all for the whole brainstorming idea," Fifi told them. "But on one condition. If you two promise to never bring up Edward having my parents killed again."

Violet looked over at Shayne, who was waving her white linen napkin in the air as if it were a flag. Fifi nodded at her, then turned to Violet.

"Fine," Violet replied as she got up and walked toward the

door. "Now decide what you'd like for lunch while I go get my laptop. That way I can take notes while we throw out ideas."

"Sounds good!" Shayne rocked back and forth three times before finally pulling herself out of her chair. "I'm thinking about baked pork chops."

"Yuck." Fifi wrinkled her nose in disgust while, following her out of the room. "How about a nice salad?"

"*Please.*"

Violet watched while her two friends headed toward the dining room, then slipped inside the library to send a quick email just to say so far, so good.

# THE PLAN

# Chapter Eight

"I got nuthin," Shayne told Fifi.

"*Nothing?*"

"Nada."

It had been a week since their gathering at Violet's house. The threesome had attempted to hold a brainstorming session during lunch, but it went awry. So Violet suggested that they go home and think on their own, then reconvene at a later date. Well, that day was today, and Shayne and Fifi were on their way to Violet's house to present their ideas.

"It's the kids' fault I don't have anything," Shayne whined. "Earlier this week I had to go to Matthew's school and talk to the principal because he doesn't want Matthew going to the prom with his boyfriend. I've spent hours on end working with Ryan on his homework, which he's having so much trouble with because of his dyslexia. I had to sit in on three therapy sessions with Cadence because of her eating disorder, I—"

"I'm sorry for what I said about your kids," Fifi blurted out. "I was just lashing out because I was upset and hurt. But I didn't mean it."

"I know you didn't. I'm sorry for what I said, too. I had no right to accuse someone you care about of doing . . . you know."

"Well, you do have a right to your opinion. But next time, just keep it to yourself!"

"I will!" Shayne laughed as they approached Violet's door and rang the bell.

"You all are going to be pleased with the ideas I came up with," Fifi said, clutching her portfolio proudly.

"Good. I wonder what Violet came up with, considering

this whole idea was her brainchild and all."

"Me, too. It should be interesting."

"Hello, ladies," Rita grunted when she threw the door open. "Miss Christianson is waiting for you in the dining room."

"Thank you." Fifi stepped inside the huge foyer, with Shayne following closely behind.

"Ooh," Shayne breathed when they entered the dining room. Violet was sitting at the head of the table, which was covered with trays of fruit, bagels, croissants, muffins, orange juice, and champagne.

"Good morning," Violet said pleasantly.

"*Hello*," Fifi sang, waving her portfolio in the air. "You ready for this?"

"I certainly am." Violet looked over at Shayne, who was busy piling food onto a plate. "Um, good *morning*."

"Oh, sorry. Hi. This spread is just so lovely . . . how are you?" she continued, her gaze still glued to the table.

"Would anyone like a mimosa?" Violet asked.

"I would!" Shayne squealed, her body jiggling as she bounced around to the bagel tray.

"Just orange juice for me," Fifi said. She prepared a small plate of fruit for herself, then sat down next to Violet. Shayne piled two huge plates high then struggled not to drop anything as she sat down across from Fifi.

Violet poured a glass of juice for Fifi, a mimosa for Shayne, and a glass of champagne for herself.

"You know that's not a mimosa," Shayne told her.

"Yes, it is. I just held the juice." Violet turned to Fifi. "So, what've you got?"

"Well," she said giddily, opening her portfolio to the first page. "I think I've got the answers to all of our problems right here in front of me. Who should I start with?"

"Let's start with me." Violet sipped from her glass and crossed her legs.

"Okay . . ." Fifi flipped through pages until she got to the one with Violet's name on top. "Here we go."

"This is so exciting," Shayne said before biting off almost half of an apple cinnamon muffin.

Violet watched as crumbs flew from her mouth. She resisted the urge to call Rita in with the Pledge and a towel and instead turned to Fifi.

"Let's start with how Elliot's no longer with us, may he rest in peace," Fifi said, her tone somber. "It's been a while since he passed, and not to be insensitive or anything, but I think it's time for you to start dating again."

"Oh, no," Shayne declared. "I don't think she's ready for that just yet."

"No, let her finish." Violet smiled clandestinely, drained her glass, then refilled it.

"*Thank* you." Fifi threw Shayne a look. "As I was saying, I think it's time for you to get out there and start meeting new people. You could start by going out to singles events, or coffee shops and bookstores, or even try Internet dating."

"I could . . ." Violet lit a cigarette and glanced down at Fifi's portfolio. "What else you got?"

"Well, the fact that you really want children is your other main issues. So I was thinking, why not adopt? There are so many kids out there who need homes, and you'd be able to provide such a wonderful and privileged life. Don't you agree?"

Violet looked over at Fifi unenthusiastically. "Is that it?"

Fifi's shoulders slumped in defeat. "No. I've got one more thing. I think you need to stop worrying so much about the legal issues regarding Elliot's business partner and just let your lawyer handle them. He's wrong, and in the end, you know you'll be vindicated, so . . ."

"Don't sound so discouraged," Violet said, reaching over and patting Fifi's arm condescendingly. "Your ideas are great. I just don't know how easy it would be to incorporate them into my plan."

"What plan?"

"We'll get to that. Tell us your ideas for Shayne."

"Yeah, my turn!" Shayne clapped her hands before piling more food onto her plate.

Fifi eyed Shayne's enormous second helping and shook her head. "As for you, I think you need to start by getting help for your food addiction."

"*Food* addiction?" The bagel Shayne was holding fell out of her hand and back down onto the tray. "I don't have a food addiction."

"Yes, you do, sweetie. Look at your plate. We haven't been here a good twenty minutes, and you're already going back for seconds."

"But I'm hungry."

"No, you're not. You're lonely and frustrated and tired. And that's totally understandable, considering what you're going through. But food isn't the answer. It's only a momentary fix, which is why you're always going back for more so quickly. In my opinion, that's a problem."

"Maybe." Shayne shrugged, sitting back down slowly. "What else?"

"I also think you should hire a nanny who could double as a housekeeper. You need help with the kids and around the house. You can't do it all by yourself. I don't even understand why you're trying to."

"Because I'd feel like a negligent parent if I didn't take care of my children myself. And nobody cleans as well as I do. Plus, I don't want anybody cleaning my toilet and washing my panties. That's personal!"

"Well, you can pick and choose what you'd have the housekeeper do. I just don't think you should continue trying to do it all on your own. You're going to run yourself ragged and end up sick. Then what good would you be to your children?"

"None," Shayne quietly said, as she stared down at her plate. "Is that it?"

"I've got one more thing for you. I think you should take up a hobby. You don't have any interests outside of your family. You need to get involved in some sort of activity, whether it be gardening, or salsa dancing, or playing tennis. I think something like that would be good for you."

"But pageantry is my passion."

"I'm talking about something you can actually participate in. Watching beauty pageants on television is not a passion. I think you need to get out of the house and get active. And now that Russell is gone, maybe you should also consider dating again."

"*Please.*" Shayne snorted before biting into a croissant. "Who would want me?"

"Plenty of men. But you need to start by getting out and making yourself available. And working on becoming the type of person you'd want to be with."

"I can't wait to hear what you've got for yourself," Shayne said sarcastically.

Fifi turned to the page with her name on top, and before she started reading, looked up at Violet. "Why are you so quiet?"

"I'm just waiting for my turn."

Shayne side-eyed Violet slyly. "You must have something serious brewing over there. Should I be afraid?"

Violet winked at Shayne then turned to Fifi. "Go ahead."

"Well, I've already put my first plan into action by enrolling in a parenting class. I also went to the bookstore yesterday and bought almost every parenting book on the shelf."

"I wish I would've done that," Shayne said. "Then maybe my family wouldn't be so screwed up now."

Violet threw Shayne a sympathetic look. "Don't do that to yourself. This is about forward movement. We're done with the past. Anything before today is irrelevant. From this moment on, we're only focusing on the solutions. That's our promise to one another. Okay?"

"Okay." Shayne stared down at her plate, then slowly pushed it off to the side.

Fifi gave her a thumbs up then continued. "As for my relationship with Edward, I can admit that I still have feelings for him. But it's time to face the fact that he doesn't feel the same way about me. So, I'm officially erasing all thoughts of us ever having a relationship."

Shayne nodded her head enthusiastically. "Good for you."

"But I am going to seek child support, and I'll always be open to him being a part of our child's life."

Shayne's eyebrows shot up toward the ceiling. "Aren't you scared?"

"Scared of what?" Fifi asked.

"I don't know," Shayne mumbled before finishing off her mimosa then sliding her glass toward Violet. "More, please. Hold the juice this time."

"Are you done, Fifi?" Violet asked as she refilled Shayne's glass.

"Yes. I'm done." She closed her portfolio slowly. "So, what do you all think?"

"I think your suggestions are . . . *good*," Violet said.

"You do? Because you didn't seem too thrilled when I was reading them off."

"Well, I guess I was expecting to hear something a little more . . . extraordinary."

"So sorry to disappoint you. What did *you* come up with?"

"Let's hear what Shayne's got first."

"I got nothing," Shayne told her.

"Why not?"

"Because of the kids."

"How did the kids keep you from—"

"Look, it's a long story," Shayne said. "I'll tell you about it later. Just go ahead with your ideas."

"Okay." Violet stood up and sauntered over to the double doors and slid them shut. "Before I start, I want to ask you both to please be extremely open-minded with what I'm about to suggest. Because my plan is a little, how should I put it, *unconventional*."

"Ooh, I can't wait," Shayne said as she rubbed her hands together and danced around in her chair.

Violet sat back down and polished off her third glass of champagne, then looked from Fifi to Shayne deviously. "You all know that I came in very close contact with a lot of the men at the prison, right?"

"Right," Shayne and Fifi said in unison.

"Well, believe it or not, I met some really decent men there."

"Decent men who worked there?" Shayne asked.

"No, decent men who were incarcerated there." Violet waited for her friends' reaction. When she didn't get one, she continued, "These men may not have been innocent, but in some cases, the crimes they committed were actually justifiable. They don't deserve to be locked up. They are good men who deserve to be free."

"*Okay*," Shayne said slowly. "But what does that have to do with our forward movement?"

"I think that if nothing else, we've established that we all need men in our lives for various reasons. But who wants to be bothered going out to happy hours and health clubs to meet men who are probably selfish, unavailable, heartless liars? I know I don't. I'd rather invest in a sure thing. A man who I can control. Who will do what I want, when I want."

Fifi snorted loudly. "That sounds good. Too bad it doesn't exist!"

Shayne nodded her head. "It certainly doesn't."

"Oh, but it does." Violet took a deep breath and squared her shoulders. "Ladies, I'm proposing that we acquire men from the prison in order to help us put our lives back together."

Shayne and Fifi stared at Violet blankly. Neither of them seemed to comprehend what she had just suggested fully.

"Think about it. If we acquire men from the prison, they'd be under our thumbs. In our control. There for our own personal fulfillment. Whenever, wherever, and however we want. Who could say no to that?"

"*I* could," Fifi declared.

Shayne held her hand up. "Me, too. And how could that possibly work anyway? There isn't much fulfilling a man could do behind bars."

"That's the thing," Violet said. "The men would no longer be behind bars. If we decide to go through with this, they would be released from prison and handed over to us."

Fifi threw her head back and laughed hysterically. "Wait, wait, wait. After referring to my ideas as *un-extraordinary*, your plan is to allow convicted criminals into our lives? That is *insane*. Not to mention there isn't a thing some idiot delinquent could do for me."

"These men are not idiots. They're smart and capable and should be put to good use. What better way to do that than to have them step in and help us?"

Fifi stared off into space. "This has got to be the craziest thing I've ever heard."

"Even if we decided to go through with this, how would

we get the men out of jail?" Shayne asked, her voice trembling with fear.

"Easy. Through my relationship with Gordon Meyers. The prison warden."

"What kind of relationship do you have with the warden that he'd just hand three criminals over to you?" Fifi asked skeptically.

Violet looked over at Fifi, her eyes twinkling cryptically "Put it this way. I know his secrets . . ."

"Wow. Those must be some serious secrets," Shayne said.

Fifi grabbed her portfolio and stood up. "I love you, Vi. But you're crazy. And I don't want any part of this."

Violet sat back in her chair and smirked at Fifi coolly. "Hold on, my pregnant little friend. Do you really want to go through the rest of your pregnancy alone? With no assistance? No protection? No one to hold you when you're feeling vulnerable? I hate to bring this up, but your parents were your main support. But they're no longer here. And I love you, but I'm not going to console you late at night because I'll be getting consoled by my inmate. And hopefully, so will Shayne. So I think you need to reconsider. Plus, there are probably a million other reasons why having a big strong man at your beck and call could benefit you."

Violet's words sat Fifi back down. She allowed her proposal to sink in. "But what if I get stuck with someone who doesn't want to assist and hold and protect me?"

"That's impossible. Because our money is going to buy us the best damn prison inmates, period. Meaning they'll have no choice but to do whatever the hell we tell them to."

"Wait, did you say *buy*?" Shayne asked, her mouth dropping so fast that her double chins shook. "As in buying these men from the prison?"

"No. We'd be buying them from the warden."

"It's tempting, Violet, I will say that." Fifi chuckled, getting back up again. "But I'm afraid I'm going to have to pass."

"Me too, Vi. I'm sorry," Shayne said, following Fifi out of the room. "I think I might take some of Fifi's ideas into consideration instead."

"You sure? All those kids and no one to help control them? No strong male presence to step in when they won't listen to you? No one to disregard your flaws and just love you for who you are?"

Shayne looked at Violet as if she wanted to reconsider, but when Fifi pulled her arm, she turned around and kept walking.

"Fine then." Violet poured herself another glass of champagne. "But I'm going to see the warden at the end of the week. So if you all change your minds, you need to let me know before then."

"Don't hold your breath," Fifi called out.

"We'll see," Violet murmured.


The minute they hit the pavement, Fifi and Shayne simultaneously took deep breaths.

"Those salsa lessons sound pretty good to you now, don't they?" Fifi asked.

"How about we get online now and find out where they're being taught?"

"Cool. I'll type up some healthy recipes for you to try and show you all of the childcare books I bought, too," Fifi responded as they headed toward her house arm-in-arm.

# CHAPTER NINE

It didn't take Fifi long to begin working on her plan. The parenting class she'd enrolled in was going great. After only a week she'd already learned every phase of a baby's development from conception to birth, the proper diet and exercise program for a pregnant woman to follow, and the difference between using a doctor versus using a midwife for a baby's delivery.

Fifi also enrolled in a Lamaze class. Unfortunately, she was the only woman in the class without a partner, since Shayne had to drop out after her hands got too full at home. But that was okay. Fifi was confident that she could learn how to breathe and push during labor and delivery on her own.

She'd also begun her letter-writing campaign seeking child support from Edward. Fifi had sent several letters via certified mail to his office as well as his home. At that point, she didn't care whether his wife found out or not. There was no hope of them ever having a real relationship, so there was no need for her to remain discreet for his sake. She no longer cared about protecting him. The only thing she cared about was providing the best possible life for her baby. Her hope was that she and the senator could come to some sort of agreement so that she wouldn't have to take it a step further and seek child support through the court.

And lastly, Fifi had hired one of the best interior decorators in town to design her baby's nursery. He'd already come up with several good ideas, and the room was set to be completed well before the baby's birth. So as far as Fifi was concerned, she was off to an amazing start.

Shayne had also begun embarking on her journey of self-improvement. She started by experimenting with several of the recipes that Fifi had given her, including the tofu burgers and zucchini chips, which the kids hated but she didn't find half bad. She'd been making a conscious effort to watch her portions and had even whittled her servings down from three to two during each meal.

Ursula, Shayne's new maid, had been in several times to clean her house. Despite the fact that Shayne had to go behind her on more than one occasion to get things just so, she seemed to be working out. And not only was Ursula's cooking delicious, but she didn't pass judgment on Shayne the few times she'd slipped up and finished off a whole meal before the kids even had a chance to eat.

As for a hobby, Shayne decided to try her hand at gardening. The only thing she'd planted so far were tomatoes, which were already beginning to grow. But she'd bought a stack of gardening magazines plus all the tools she needed, and her plan was to have a backyard so filled with vegetables that she'd never have to walk down a produce aisle again.

And lastly, in an attempt to meet the man of her dreams, Shayne posted a dating profile on *www.find-a-mate.com*. She did shave a few years off of her age, a few pounds off of her weight, and upload a photo that was over ten years old. But that was okay because she planned to have some weight off by the time she began communicating with someone and actually had to meet him. And if necessary, she could always take Violet up on her offer and pay her plastic surgeon a visit.

After a long discussion with one another, Shayne and Fifi both agreed that they were doing just fine on their own. They didn't need Violet's obscure plan to help get their lives together. All they needed was a set of effective, realistic goals, some self-motivation, and each other.

But then one night, Fifi called Shayne in an utter panic. She explained how she'd been relaxing in her den while working on a quiz in one of her parenting books when she heard car tires screech loudly in front of her house. Fifi jumped up to see if one of her neighbors had gotten into an accident. Right before she stepped into the living room, a round of ear-piercing ammunition blasted through her picture window. Fifi screamed and fell to the floor. She covered her ears as another round of ammunition shot through the dining room window. She crawled back into the den and called 9-1-1. The dispatcher said they'd send someone over immediately. But the police never showed up.

Shane insisted that Fifi spend the night at her house that evening, and the two friends didn't return to Fifi's house until the window repairmen arrived the next afternoon to clean up the mess and replace the glass. When the men were leaving, Shayne and Fifi noticed a suspicious black *Town Car* with black tinted windows parked at the end of the block. They hurried back inside the house and locked every door. Before Fifi could pick up the phone to call the police, it rang. She tapped the speaker button, and a sinister voice spewed, "Kill it before I kill you." Then the phone went dead. Fifi screamed, and she and Shayne ran back to Shayne's house as fast as they could.

Things hadn't been going much better for Shayne, either. She had to fire Ursula after she'd caught her coming on to Matthew. And speaking of Matthew, Shayne's cousin called and told her that he was supposedly dating some Brazilian male porn star. The kids at school were making fun of Ryan's dyslexia so badly that he was threatening to drop out. Cadence had to be rushed to the hospital a few days ago after overdosing on laxatives. And Shayne's garden had been ruined after she'd found her neighbor's dead dog lying in a pool of blood over her tomatoes. She suspected Basil had something to do with it, as did the neighbors, who were threatening to press charges.

And lastly, only one man had responded to Shayne's profile on find-a-mate.com. But he seemed so strange and creepy that she decided to *Google* his name just to see what would come up. Low and behold, he was a registered sex offender.

Just when Shayne was heading to her bathroom to grab a razor blade and end it all, her phone rang.

"Hello?"

"*Shayne!*" It was Fifi, who'd gone back home that morning. "The voice just called again. This time it said, *Is it dead yet? If not, you will be tonight.*"

"Oh, God," Shayne moaned.

"My plan isn't working."

"I know. Your plan isn't working for me, either."

"Are you thinking what I'm thinking?"

"I think so."

Fifi sighed. "I guess I'll call Violet and set up a meeting for tomorrow."

"But what if we're too late?" Shayne cried. "She probably went to see the warden and already has her inmate!"

"Please. Violet was bluffing. If she were serious about going through with the plan without us, she would've had us meet in the library instead of the dining room. She thinks it's bad luck to close deals anywhere except the library."

"You think?"

"I know," Fifi said. "And because I'm sure she doesn't want to do this alone, Violet's probably been waiting by the phone for us to call and give her the green light."

"Good, because I'm ready to."

"So am I."

"Then let's do it."

"Hold on." Fifi switched over onto the other line to conference Violet in.

# CHAPTER TEN

"Ladies," Violet said to Shayne and Fifi the next day when they entered her library. She was sitting behind her huge teakwood desk, motioning for them to sit down across from her.

Violet was dressed in a conservative black pantsuit. Her hair was pulled back in a severe bun. She had on very little makeup. Her jewelry consisted only of diamond studs in her ears and a thin platinum band on her ring finger. She wasn't swirling a cocktail in one hand and clutching a cigarette in the other. There were no refreshments in sight. Only a crystal pitcher filled with ice water sitting in the middle of the desk.

Fifi pulled Shayne's arm, and they both proceeded to sit down. Violet filled their glasses, a smug smirk spread across her face.

"How have you two been?" she asked.

"Fine," Fifi said.

"Not good," Shayne uttered simultaneously.

Violet looked up at them, struggling to conceal her laughter. "Well, which is it? Fine or not good?"

Fifi sighed deeply, then looked down at her belly and covered it with her hands. "Not good. Edward has been calling and threatening to kill me if I don't terminate the pregnancy. He also had my living and dining room windows ambushed."

"You know, come to think of it, I did hear some loud noise coming from your house the other night," Violet replied haughtily, swiveling back and forth in her chair. "And Shayne? What about you?"

"Well, I had to fire the maid I'd just hired because she was hitting on Matthew, who by the way is supposedly dating some male porn star. Ryan wants to drop out of school, Cadence was released from the hospital yesterday after OD'ing on laxatives, Basil killed the neighbor's dog, a sex offender emailed me—"

Violet held up her hand. "Enough said." She reached inside a manila folder and pulled three sheets of paper out. Then she folded her hands and looked up at her friends. "Are you two ready?"

"Yes," Shayne and Fifi said in unison as they slid to the edge of their seats.

"All right then. Over the past couple of weeks, as I waited for the two of you to come to your senses, I began reviewing my prison inmate files and audiotapes. I already had a few men in mind, but I just wanted to make sure I was on the right track in choosing who would be most suitable for each of us. So, this is what I came up with."

Shayne swallowed several gulps of water so quickly that she visibly choked. Fifi closed her eyes and wrapped her arms around her stomach as if to protect her unborn child from what she was about to hear.

"Shayne?" Violet said.

She jumped in her seat and spilled water down the front of her powder blue velour tracksuit.

Violet chuckled. "Are you okay?"

"Y-yes. I'm fine. Just a little . . . nervous."

"Don't be." Violet picked up one of the papers that she'd pulled from the folder. "This is going to be good for you. For all of us. You'll see." She smiled sweetly, then began reading. "Shayne, I'm recommending that you purchase inmate number zero-five-five-two-one, Conrad Tate."

"Conrad Tate," Shayne repeated, her eyes fixated on the paper as if it were Conrad himself.

"Yes. Conrad was convicted of identity theft back in two-thousand-fifteen—"

"Whose identity did he steal?" Shayne asked.

"I'd rather not say right now. That information is strictly confidential, so I won't elaborate on the details until the negotiations have been completed and the contracts are signed."

"Contracts? What contracts?" Shayne asked.

Fifi's gazed shifted from Shayne to Violet. "Wait a minute. You actually expect us to go through with this without even knowing these criminals' full backgrounds? Why would we do that? It's absurd."

"Why wouldn't you do it? What other option do you have? To keep taking your classes and reading your books until you get murdered just like your . . ." Violet paused, then rephrased her question. "Until you get murdered before your baby is even born?"

"Watch it," Fifi said firmly, pointing at Violet.

"Look. All I'm asking is that you accept what I can tell you for now and let me disclose everything else once the deals are done."

"This is not a real estate deal, Violet," Fifi said. "These men aren't properties. They're human beings who are capable of doing — "

"Whatever the hell we tell them to. And no, this isn't a real estate deal, but it *is* business. Just as I own property that I profit from monetarily, I'll be owning a man who I will profit from in whatever ways I see fit."

"This just doesn't seem right," Shayne said, squirming in her seat.

"Neither do dead dogs and sex offenders, now do they?"

"That wasn't necessary," Fifi told Violet.

"The truth is always necessary. Now, may I proceed?"

Shayne and Fifi fell silent for several moments before Shayne finally spoke up. "Go ahead."

"Thank you." Violet looked back down at her paper and

continued reading. "Conrad Tate is forty-five-years old. He worked in construction before his arrest. He's never been married and doesn't have any children. As for his appearance, he's six-three, has dirty blond hair, blue-green eyes, sun-kissed skin, a young Robert Redford-type face, and a good body. As for his personality, he's a kind, capable, strong man who's smart and very family-oriented. As for his sentence, Conrad's due to be released in twenty-twenty-five unless you go through with this plan and get him out now."

Shayne poured herself another glass of water and gulped it down quickly. "I must admit, Conrad does sound appealing. No doubt he'll be better than *Captain Long Shlong* from find-a-mate-dot-com.

"So then, what do you think?" Violet asked.

"I think I just may be able to do this. Maybe . . ."

"Shayne, I wouldn't steer you wrong. Conrad really is a great guy. After the deal is complete, I'll even let you listen to a couple of the audiotapes from his counseling sessions so that you can hear for yourself."

"Do you have a picture of him?"

"Unfortunately, I don't. But trust me, he's very attractive. Grade A perfection. I wouldn't have you spend your money on anything less."

Fifi burst out laughing. "Do you *hear* yourself?"

"Yes, I do. I hear myself sounding like quite the businesswoman."

"More like a cattlewoman," Shayne said.

"Well," Fifi chimed in, "Let's hear who you've got for me."

Violet slid a piece of paper from underneath her pile. "Fifi, for you I've chosen inmate number six-three-zero-four-two, Bodie Jacobs. Bodie was convicted of first-degree murder back in two-thousand-ten."

Fifi's head fell in shock. "*What*! Violet. You can't be serious. A convicted murderer? You've chosen a convicted *murderer* for me?"

"Keep in mind there's more information to be had once the deal closes."

"He kills people! What more do I need to know?"

"The circumstances, perhaps? Maybe it was self-defense. Maybe it was an accident. Maybe it was well-deserved. And if I were you, I wouldn't mind having a convicted killer around, considering what's been going on."

Fifi sat quietly for a moment, then crossed her arms. "Continue."

"Bodie is thirty-five-years-old and was dishonorably discharged from the Marines back in the mid-two-thousands. Before his arrest, he was pursuing a career in architectural engineering. He's never been married and doesn't have children. As for his appearance, he's five-eleven, has thick dark hair, bright brown eyes, a boyishly cute face, and a lean muscular body. As for his personality, he's boisterous, thoughtful, and a deep thinker. He's also a bit temperamental at times, but only because he's so passionate about the things he believes in."

"He sounds like a goddamn maniac," Fifi muttered under her breath. Violet ignored her and kept reading.

"As for his sentence? Life. Unless of course you go through with this."

"If I do, I'd love to know how you're going to pull it off."

"The less you know, the better," Violet told her. "Just trust me, Fifi. I know what I'm doing."

"You'd better, because I'd hate to be around if this plan goes awry. These men could hurt us, or we could go to jail ourselves. I don't know . . ."

"It won't go awry because my plan is airtight, and I do not fail."

"We know you don't, Vi," Shayne said. "Why don't you go ahead and tell us about your inmate."

Violet looked at Fifi and raised her eyebrows, questioning whether or not she too wanted to hear about him.

Fifi sighed heavily. "Go ahead."

"So, last but not least, I have selected for myself inmate number nine-two-five-three-seven, BJ Ellis. BJ is thirty-nine-years old and was convicted of racketeering back in twenty-thirteen. He's married and has a daughter and two sons."

"So you're buying a man who has a family?" Shayne asked. "How's that going to work?"

"Trust me, it'll work. Now, as for his looks, BJ is five-nine, has curly black hair, olive skin, a pudgy but handsome enough face, and a bit of a potbelly. But his personality more than makes up for his physique. BJ is one of the smartest, funniest, most well-adjusted men I've ever met. His parents died when he was ten years old, so their neighbors who lived across the street adopted him. The family happened to be involved in organized crime, which is how BJ ended up getting involved in racketeering. He's serving a fifteen-year sentence, but hopefully not for long after I meet with the warden tomorrow."

"You're meeting with the warden *tomorrow*?" Shayne asked.

"Yes. Which is why we need to get this wrapped up today. Each of these descriptions also serves as the contract, with a disclaimer, terms of agreement, and place to sign down at the bottom."

Violet placed Fifi and Shayne's inmate information in front of them. Fifi grabbed the paper and began reading. After several minutes, she rolled her eyes and looked up at Violet.

"So if something happens to one of us, you're claiming no responsibility?"

"Yes. This is strictly a suggestion from me to you. I'm not forcing you to do anything. I'm only recommending it. If you choose to participate, you'd be doing so at your own risk."

"And you want us to call you first before calling the police if something goes wrong?" Shayne asked.

"Yes."

"Say if, I don't know, this Bodie kills my baby or something, I'm supposed to call you instead of the police?" Fifi asked.

"Yes. Do you understand the ramifications of what we're doing here? News flash! This shit is illegal. In the event that something goes wrong, I would need to contact the warden and have him handle it."

"Oh, okay. So while I'm crying over my dead baby's body, I'm supposed to wait for you to call the warden and explain to him what happened so that he can sit with his thumb up his ass trying to figure out what to do? Yeah, *that* makes sense. I'd much rather let the police handle it."

"Well, how would you handle explaining to the police that you got together with your girlfriends and blackmailed the warden of the state prison into letting you buy an inmate for yourself, which is how he got inside of your house to kill your baby in the first place? And speaking of the police, weren't they the ones sitting with their thumbs up their asses the night you were crying over your shattered windows?"

Fifi stared at Violet indignantly. Violet tilted her head to the side and stared right back at her. Fifi surrendered first.

"Exactly how much is this going to cost us?" she asked.

"I don't know yet. I'll negotiate the price with the warden tomorrow after I tell him about the plan. If either of you can't cover the full cost, I'll put up whatever you need."

Shayne dug inside her purse and pulled out a pen. She scribbled her name on the bottom of the contract, handed it back to Violet, then turned to Fifi.

"You know how a strange opportunity can sometimes fall in your lap, and while you may not understand it at the time, you go ahead and take advantage of it and discover its full purpose afterward?"

Fifi stared down at the contract and nodded her head.

"Well, this is that opportunity. We tried your plan, and it failed. This may be our last chance to crawl out of the holes we've stumbled into before something really catastrophic happens. And believe me, that catastrophe is right around the corner, just waiting for us to walk out of here without signing these contracts."

Fifi's eyes filled with tears when Shayne handed her the pen.

"Sign it," she said softly.

Fifi's hand shook as she took the pen and signed her name on the dotted line. Tears fell from her eyes and smeared the ink that spelled out her illegible signature. She picked up the contract and handed it to Violet. "I somehow feel like I'm signing my soul over to the devil."

"I've been called worse." Violet smiled, signing her own contract then putting all three of them inside her briefcase.

"Well, I don't know about you two, but I feel great," Shayne said, standing up and stretching her arms. "I can't wait to meet Conrad."

"What are you going to tell your kids?" Fifi asked while Violet handed her a tissue.

"I don't know. Maybe that he's my long-lost cousin? Old high school sweetheart? I'm sure I'll think of something. But my kids are so wrapped up in their own little messes that they probably won't even notice him."

"The good thing is he'll be there to help you clean up all their little messes," Violet said, getting up and walking over to the door. "Now, if you'll both follow me, Rita has a celebratory feast awaiting us in the dining room."

"Yippee!" Shayne cheered, jumping up and down and practically running out of the room.

Before Violet walked out, Fifi grabbed her arm. "I'm

scared," she whispered.

"Don't be." Violet hugged her tightly. "The scary part is about to be over. You won't have to be in that big house alone anymore. You'll have someone there to keep you company, console you, and most importantly, protect you."

"You do understand that regardless of what that contract says, I'm going to blame you if this goes wrong."

"I know you will." Violet wrapped her arm around Fifi's shoulder and led her down the hall. "But I promise you that's not going to happen. In the end, you'll be thanking me instead."

"I'd better be," Fifi replied as she entered the dining room. Shayne was already sitting down, hovering over two huge plates of food.

"My God," Violet murmured. "I'd better pay the warden a little something extra just so he can put a rush on getting those inmates to us."

"Please do," Fifi said.

"Go ahead and eat," Violet told her as she walked over to the bar and fixed herself a drink. Then she sat down at the head of the table, lit a cigarette, and began telling her friends about all the different ways Elliot's business partner Thomas was trying to swindle her now.

# THE EXECUTION

# CHAPTER ELEVEN

"Violet! It's so good to see you," Gordon Meyers, the prison warden, said when she strolled into his office. He got up from his desk, looking just as fat and jolly as ever, and bounced over toward her.

"Good to see you too, Gordon." Violet embraced him tightly. "It's been too long."

"It certainly has. You look just as beautiful as ever. That dress always was my favorite on you."

"Was it?" Violet asked sweetly, having worn the beige *Chanel* for that very reason.

"It sure was." Gordon ran his rough, chubby hand down her back and pulled out a chair. "Please, have a seat."

"Thank you." Violet sat down and crossed her legs, watching as Gordon wobbled over to the other side of the desk. He plopped down into his chair, licking his chapped lips and staring at her.

"You know the boys still ask about you all the time. They're waiting for you to come back to us. They miss you immensely. As do I."

"I miss them, too. Which is sort of why I'm here."

"Oh?" Gordon clapped his plump hands. "Does that mean you're coming back?"

"Not exactly. I'm actually here to present you with a business proposition."

"Well, I do like to consider myself a bona fide businessman. Let's see, I own two houses that I rent to underprivileged families, my brother and I are looking to open a towing company, and—"

Violet cleared her throat impatiently. "Good then. That means you'll be in total agreement with this opportunity of mine."

"Great." Gordon grinned, his thick tongue sticking out from between his pointy gray teeth. "Let's hear it."

"Well, as you know, I've been alone since Elliot's death."

Gordon's expression turned somber. "I know. I'm so sorry about that."

"Thank you. It has been difficult, and I'm having a hard time holding everything together. I need help."

"Of course. Is there anything I can do?"

"As a matter of fact, there is," Violet said, pausing for the dramatic effect.

"What is it?" Gordon leaned into the desk so hard that it split his breasts in half. "Anything you need, just name it."

"Anything?"

"Anything."

"All right then." Violet sat straight up and looked Gordon directly in the eye. "I would like to buy an inmate from you."

Gordon sat silently for several moments before removing his thick gold-rimmed bifocals. "Excuse me?"

"I said I would like to buy an inmate from you. Three, actually. One for me and two others for my friends."

Gordon stared at Violet with a blank expression on his face, then blinked rapidly. "I'm sorry. You said you want to buy . . . *inmates* from me?"

"Yes." She smiled sweetly.

"For what?"

"That's personal."

"It's . . . personal?"

"Yes. Personal."

"I don't think I'm understanding you."

"Yes, you are," Violet said, her smile tightening.

"You're right. I do understand you. What I meant to say was I don't think I can help you."

Her tight smile faded. "Yes, you can."

"How?"

"By selling the inmates to me."

"And how would I go about doing that?" Gordon asked, chuckling softly.

"By telling me how much they'd cost and signing a contract stating that you agreed to my terms and conditions."

"Violet," Gordon wheezed, rolling his chair away from the desk. "You know you're asking me to do something that I can't make happen. And if you wanna know what I think, I think your request is ridiculous. What do you want with convicted felons anyway?"

Violet uncrossed her legs and rolled her chair closer to the desk. "First of all, I'm asking you to do something that you can definitely make happen. Secondly, I, in fact, don't want to know what you think, and third, it's none of your business what I want with convicted felons." She pulled a folder out of her briefcase and sat it on the desk. "Your only business is to sign this contract, turn the inmates over to me then cash your check."

Gordon laughed heartily. "You know Violet, I always knew there was something wrong with you. There always is when it comes to women as beautiful as you."

Violet held her hand to her face and snickered. "My goodness. What a backhanded compliment that was."

"Take it however you'd like." Gordon stood up and hobbled over to the door, this time with his cane in tow. "It was good seeing you, darling. I'm glad you came by to pay me a visit. But I'm going to have to turn down that business proposition of yours and ask you to leave. I've got a lot of work to do."

Violet turned and looked at Gordon as he opened the door. She made sure her expression was grim, her eyes cold. "Sit back down, Mr. Meyers."

"Oh, now you wanna get formal, huh?" Gordon said,

laughing so hard that he began to choke on phlegm. "Violet, I asked you to leave nicely. Please do so before I have one of the guards escort you out of here in a not-so-nice manner."

"Mr. Meyers, I asked you to sit back down nicely. Please do so before I talk some of your prisoners into pressing charges against you." Violet turned back around in her chair, crossed her legs again and pulled a cigarette out of her beige *Chanel* clutch.

Gordon froze, then closed the door slowly and shuffled back over to his desk. "You know there's no smoking in here."

"Really?" Violet lit her cigarette and blew smoke in his face.

Gordon pulled a mustard stained handkerchief out of his pocket and patted the thick droplets of sweat that had begun forming on his spotted forehead. "Why would any of my boys want to press charges against me?"

"Oh, come on, do I really need to answer that question?"

"Actually . . . yes. Because I have no idea what you're talking about."

"Have you forgotten the type of work I did here? I was a psychiatrist, Gordon. My job was to sit and listen to prisoners' problems and issues and fears all day. Everyday."

"And you were so *good* at—"

"Please don't start kissing my ass. It's so unbecoming. Just look over this contract, sign it, negotiate the cost of three inmates, and let me go on about my day."

Gordon's eyes filled with hurt as he took the contract and began reading it. But after several moments he shoved it back at Violet, his eyes now filled with rage.

"I will not do this. There is no way I will do this. I've run this prison for over thirty years, and not once have I done or been asked to do anything this outrageous." Gordon inhaled deeply and exhaled a puff of hot, odorous breath before continuing. "You can't threaten me, either. Because you will never get close enough to my inmates to persuade them to do anything against me. As a matter of fact, I'm going to have you banned from this prison altogether. Now get out!"

Violet watched him turn away from her. She threw her head back and laughed, put her cigarette out on his desk, and snapped her fingers in his face.

Gordon jumped and turned back slowly, looking at her through the corner of his eye.

"Do you know who I am, sweetie?" she asked. "Are you aware of how much money I have? I could buy this goddamn prison if I wanted to. Lucky for you, I don't. Now I didn't want to get dirty with your fat, sweaty, smelly ass, but you're leaving me no choice. So let's go."

Gordon's eyes widened. His mouth fell open, but before he could speak, Violet continued, "If you don't sell me the three inmates that I'm requesting, I will first go to Carl Dixon and have him press charges against you for forcing him to crawl underneath this desk and suck your puny, flaccid little dick until you shot your nasty, funky spunk inside his mouth and beat him in the head until he swallowed it."

Violet smiled slightly at the sight of Gordon gripping his chest while emitting a shock-filled wheeze.

"Then I'll go to Myron Simmons and have him press charges against you for all the times you balled your stubby, elfish fingers into a fist and forced it up his ass until he bled. Then I'll have Kevin Martin tell the authorities how you forced him to lie across this floor and pull his shirt up while you squatted your hairy, portly ass over him and defecated all over his body, then had the audacity to rub the shit in. Once I'm done with him, I'll go to—"

"Okay! Okay!" Gordon yelled, his gut jiggling as he sobbed in his hands. "Just tell me what to do."

"It's all laid out in the contract." Violet pulled out another cigarette along with her sterling silver flask in victory.

"I'm t-t-too upset to read. Just t-t-tell me!"

Violet started Gordon off by having him sign the contract. Then she explained how the files for BJ Ellis, Conrad Tate, and Bodie Jacobs needed to be altered to reflect that their parole hearings were coming up immediately. Then he'd need to make sure the right people made it onto the parole board and have the three inmates released to her as soon as possible.

"Now, how much will I owe you?" Violet asked Gordon as he blew his nose.

He looked at her pitifully, his burgundy eyes practically swollen shut. "Every bit of your silence."

# THE PREPARATION

# CHAPTER TWELVE

"It's done," Violet said to Shayne and Fifi over speakerphone. She was lying in her huge marble jacuzzi with the jets turned up full blast. She was so beside herself that she was drinking her most expensive champagne straight out of the bottle.

"It is? I'm so excited!" Shayne screamed so loudly that Violet heard her kids tell her to shut up in the background.

"Believe it or not, so am I," Fifi chimed in. "I'm sick of being in this house alone. Every time the phone rings, I jump. I'm afraid to walk past the windows. I look for that black *Town Car* every time I step outside. I'm going crazy."

"Well, I'm glad you're excited now," Violet said. "I was worried you weren't going to go through with this."

"I was worried the warden was going to tear that contract up in your face and laugh you out of the jail!" Fifi said.

"Oh, believe me, he wanted to. But with everything I've got on him, he had no choice but to honor my request."

"I'd love to know what went on in that office."

"But as you both know . . ."

"The less we know, the better," Shayne and Fifi said in unison.

"Exactly."

"So, what's next?" Shayne asked. "When are the inmates going to be released? And how much are they going to cost us?"

"First, the warden has to have the information in the inmates' files changed so that they can go before the parole board and be released. I'm expecting that to happen within the next couple of weeks. As for the cost of the inmates, we're getting them for free."

"Wait, did you say *free*?" Fifi said.

"Yes. Free."

"How did that happen?" Shayne asked. "I was expecting to have to clean out my bank account for this."

"I think I overwhelmed the warden so badly with my threats that he couldn't even think about money. All he wants in return is my silence."

"Violet Christianson, you're a bad, bad girl," Fifi replied. "But I'm glad I'm getting my man for free, because all my money needs to go toward my baby. Especially since I may not be getting child support."

"We'll see about that."

"So how are we going to get the men once they're released?" Shayne asked.

"Each of the inmates is going to be released on a different day so that things won't look too obvious. I'm going to send a different car each time someone is released, and I want all of us to be there every time. During the ride home, I want things to be really relaxed, since they won't really know what's going on yet. We'll just have chit-chatty small talk until we get to my house. Once we get here, we'll have lunch, and then I'll outline what this is all about and lay down the ground rules. You two need to decide what you do and don't want and be ready to present it at that time."

"Okay, the fact that this is really about to happen is making me nervous," Fifi told them.

"I know!" Shayne chimed in. "I hope Conrad doesn't make me feel all icky and uncomfortable."

"Conrad is going to put you right at ease," Violet said.

"Now that we've signed our contracts, are you going to give us the rest of the information about the crimes they committed?" Shayne asked.

"You know what?" Fifi said. "At this point, I don't even wanna know. If I hear something I don't like, I'm going to end up regretting this. And since it's too late to turn back now, I'm just going to meet Bodie and judge him for myself."

"That's a good idea," Shayne declared. "I don't want to know either."

"And if you do at a later date, you can always just ask them."

"Let me ask you all this," Shayne said. "What are you going to do with your inmate once you get him home? And in the days and weeks to come?"

"I've been too scared to even think about it," Fifi responded.

"I'm going to start by giving BJ a tour of the house and getting him settled into the room I've prepared for him," Violet said. "I've alerted my staff that my long-lost cousin is coming to stay with me for a while. I stole that idea from you, Shayne. As for BJ's overall purpose, I'm mainly going to use him for companionship and to help with some of the business."

"You're comfortable with him getting involved in your business with those racketeering charges?" Fifi asked.

"Oh, I'm not worried about that. BJ and I grew really close when I was working at the prison, so I don't think he'd do anything underhanded to me. Plus, he'll know that I'm the reason he's out of jail, so I'm the reason he could go right back in."

"What about the personal fulfillment aspect since he's . . . you know . . . married and all," Shayne said.

"I don't plan on having sex with him, if that's what you're asking. As a matter of fact, when I'm done with him, I'm going to arrange to have him reunite with his family."

"Why would you choose a man you couldn't have sex with?" Fifi probed.

"Because there are more important things to this than sex."

"Well, I'm gonna be sleeping with Conrad!" Shayne

proclaimed. "I'm taking full advantage of this. I haven't had a man touch me in so long I forgot what it feels like."

"What about you, Fifi?" Violet asked. "You think you're gonna be giving it up to Bodie?"

"Are you kidding? My sex drive is at an all-time low. My nose is spreading, feet are beginning to swell, and my stomach is out to here. I've never felt so undesirable in my entire life."

"Oh Fifi, don't talk about yourself like that," Shayne said. "Pregnant women are beautiful."

"They are," Violet agreed. "I knew first-hand during my brief pregnancy all those years ago . . ."

Shayne and Fifi fell silent. Violet polished off her bottle of champagne and stepped out of the jacuzzi.

"Well, as long as my inmate is willing to answer my phone and guard the door," Fifi said in what appeared to be an attempt to shift the conversation, "Then he'll be all right with me."

"Where's he gonna sleep?" Shayne asked.

"I guess down in the basement. My parents had it remodeled a couple of years ago, and it's really nice. Plus, there's a bathroom and kitchenette down there, so it'll be like his own little apartment."

"Basil!" Shayne screamed. "Girls, I gotta go. My son just walked in here with about fifteen of his friends, and it looks like the gates of hell just opened in my living room."

"I need to go, too," Violet said. "My masseur is downstairs waiting for me."

"Okay, so Violet, you'll call us the minute you hear from the warden?" Fifi asked.

"The second I hear from him."

"Great. I'm getting excited again!" Shayne said.

"Good. We'll talk soon," Violet said before hanging up the phone. As she headed downstairs to the sunroom, she wondered just how much of the real plan she should share with her friends.

# THE HOMECOMING

# CHAPTER THIRTEEN

Violet stared out of the limousine's back window. She watched from a distance as her gardener Roger pulled his electric blue El Camino in front of the prison. He was posing as the pick-up for Conrad, who was the first inmate being released. Once in Roger's car, Conrad would be given a brief explanation as to what was going on while being driven down the street to the limo, where Violet, Shayne, and Fifi awaited him.

When Conrad walked out of the gate, he stood and stared at Roger. Roger gestured for him to get inside the car, then began talking and pointing toward the limo. Conrad looked up at it, then shook his head as Roger pulled off.

"Okay, here they come," Violet said, turning in her seat and looking at Shayne and Fifi. Shayne's expression was filled with terror, while Fifi's was full of uncertainty.

"I'm so scared," Shayne said as she rubbed her hands vigorously over her thighs.

"You'll be fine," Violet told her. "Just turn on that sweet charm of yours. I'm sure it'll make Conrad feel right at home."

"I hope so . . ." Shayne had traded in her sweats and Nikes for a pale pink cashmere sweater set, a soft suede gray skirt, and gray stiletto pumps. She'd had her hair stylist, who she hadn't been to in months, coif her blonde locks into a sophisticated up-do, and even had her makeup professionally done.

Fifi looked over at Shayne and shook her head. "I'm so glad you're going first."

"Ha! Thanks for the encouragement." Shayne stared out the window anxiously, watching Roger pull up behind the limo.

"Here he comes!" Violet said.

Conrad stepped out of the El Camino dressed in a navy-blue shirt, jeans, and cowboy boots. A duffle bag was thrown over his shoulder. His blondish-brown hair was neatly trimmed. His blue-green eyes were twinkling with curiosity.

"He's so handsome," Shayne breathed as the driver got out and opened the back door for him. She inhaled deeply and began fanning herself.

Violet watched as Conrad bent down and looked inside the car. First, he eyed Shayne, who was now jiggling her legs nervously. Then he glanced over at Fifi, who smiled awkwardly and waved hello. And finally, he looked over in the far corner and locked eyes with Violet.

"What the . . ." he said before finally getting inside. As soon as the driver closed the door, he yelled, "Miss Christianson! What are you doing here? What the hell's going on?"

"Hello, Conrad." Violet reached over and hugged him. "How are you?"

"I'm great! But extremely confused. Because out of nowhere I was brought before the parole board much sooner than I was supposed to be and let out of prison way before my release date. With no explanation whatsoever."

"It's a long story, Conrad. We're on the way to my house now, and once we get there, I'll let you in on exactly what's going on. In the meantime, I'd like to introduce you to two of my dearest friends, Shayne Wentworth and Fifi Gentry."

"Ladies," Conrad said, reaching out and shaking their hands.

Shayne had been holding her breath ever since he'd gotten in the car, and she didn't exhale until he took her hand in his.

Violet observed Shayne's schoolgirl behavior and snickered softly. "Would you like something to drink?" she asked Conrad. "A Heineken perhaps?"

"Absolutely. You've got a good memory."

Violet opened a bottle of beer and handed it to him. "Just wait until you see what we're having for lunch."

Conrad broke out into a huge grin, then stared up at the sunroof. "God, what did I do to deserve this?"

"It isn't what you've done, it's what you're going to do. Being a good person is what got you out of jail. Cooperating with us is what will keep you out."

Conrad looked from Violet to Fifi, then locked gazes with Shayne. "Whatever you want from me, it won't be a problem."

"Good," Violet replied as she poured glasses of champagne for herself and her two friends. She raised her flute for a toast. "Shall we? Shayne, why don't you do the honors."

Shayne batted her lashes bashfully and looked down at her lap, then took a deep breath and held her head up. "To the future. May it bring about change, happiness, and most importantly, a successful alliance."

"Hear, hear," Conrad said before smiling at her, taking a swig of beer then turning to Violet. "Well, since we can't discuss what this is all about, why don't you tell me how you've been since your husband passed away, and you left the prison?"

"Whew, now that's a long story. But here goes . . ."


As Violet continued, Shayne held her hand to her chest. She smiled slightly, her head falling to one side while watching Conrad. She slowly rocked back and forth while vigorously fanning her face.

Fifi looked over and saw Shayne's eyes roll back slightly. "Are you all right?" she whispered.

Shayne patted her forehead with the back of her hand. "I'm fine. Just a little hot."

"Well, hang in there. We're almost at Violet's."

Shayne glanced over at Conrad, who gave her a sexy smile and wink. Shayne broke out into a fit of giggles, winked back, then passed out.

"Is she coming to?" Shayne heard Fifi ask wearily.

"It looks like it," Violet replied.

"Yeah, I think she's almost with us," Shayne heard. That was the voice that opened her eyes — because it was Conrad's.

"Hey there," he said when she looked at him.

"Hi." Shayne glanced around the room, realizing that she was lying in bed inside one of Violet's guest bedrooms. "What happened?"

Fifi reached down and placed her hand on Shayne's shoulder. "Let's just say you got really . . . hot in the limo on the way here."

"And then you just passed out," Violet said.

Conrad took Shayne's hand in his. "But you're going to be fine."

His rough but warm skin felt magnificent. So magnificent that Shayne sat right up in bed, which was when she realized that all she was wearing up top was her pink lace bra.

"Oh my," Shayne gasped, quickly pulling the bedspread up over herself. "Where are my clothes?"

"Hanging in the closet," Violet replied, tightening her lips in what looked like an attempt to control her laughter.

"You were soaking wet by the time we got here," Fifi said, "So we took them off."

Conrad just stood there with an amused expression on his face.

"I'm glad to see I didn't offend anyone," Shayne said, eyeing him coyly.

"You certainly didn't," he said.

"So how long was I out?"

"Quite a while," Violet told her.

"Did I miss anything?"

"Quite a bit," Fifi responded.

"I did? What?"

"For starters, you missed a great lunch," Conrad said as he patted his stomach. "Filet mignon with grilled shiitake mushrooms, double baked potatoes, asparagus spears with cream sauce, freshly baked rolls, apple pie ala mode, and a wonderful merlot."

"That sounds delicious," Shayne said, even though food was the last thing on her mind. She looked around the group, waiting for them to continue. When they didn't, she did. "So what else did I miss? Did you all talk about . . . the plan?"

"We did," Violet responded. "We explained to Conrad the details of our plan, and we're happy to report that he loves the idea of being transferred from the big house to the Wentworth house."

"You are?" Shayne asked him.

"Absolutely. I'm ecstatic, actually. We're gonna get that household of yours straightened up in no time."

"I don't know about all that," Shayne muttered.

"We didn't quite tell Conrad the specifics of what you and the kids are dealing with," Fifi told her. "We thought we'd leave that up to you."

"That's fine." But in reality, Shayne wished her friends would've shared the gory details so that she wouldn't have to face the embarrassment of doing it herself.

"Conrad, would you please excuse us?" Violet asked. "We're going to get Shayne dressed, then we'll meet you back downstairs."

"Of course." Conrad reached down and gently touched Shayne's arm. "I'm glad you're okay."

"Thank you." The minute he was out of the room, Shayne murmured, "I think I'm in love . . ."

Violet folded her arms. "So we see!"

"And from the looks of things, Conrad is, too," Fifi said.

"You think so?" Shayne asked eagerly.

"Oh, I know so. You should've seen the look on his face when we told him what the stipulations of his being released from jail are. When he heard he'd be living with you as an employee of sorts, he practically leaped out of his chair."

"Are you serious?" Shayne hopped up out of bed and slipped on her clothes.

"Why would you expect anything else?" Violet asked.

"Because . . . I'm not the girl I used to be, let's just say that."

Fifi threw her arms up over her head. "Meaning you're not a pageant girl anymore? Who cares? You're still the same person. And you're still beautiful."

Shayne snorted. "Yeah, and fat as hell."

"You're far from fat," Violet said. "You're voluptuous."

"That's the word the media always uses to describe fat actresses."

"And the media considers actresses fat if they're over a size two. So, what's your point?"

"Now that you put it that way, I guess I don't have one." Shayne walked over to the mirror and touched up her hair and makeup. "But that doesn't change the fact that I'm fat."

Fifi walked up behind Shayne and tucked the tag inside her sweater. "Russell sucked every ounce of self-esteem out of you, didn't he?"

"I hate to admit it, but yes, he did. Imagine someone telling you that you were disgusting and revolting enough to turn him asexual. Believe me, you'd be lacking self-esteem, too."

"Well, the man I loved whose child I'm having is threatening my life, which isn't exactly a confidence booster. But I'm not letting it get me down."

Violet strolled across the room. "And let's not even get into the child that my dead husband's whore will be giving birth to soon. There's nothing more humiliating than your husband having an affair, but I'm not letting that get me down, either. Instead, I'm getting even, along with my two best friends."

"Getting even?" Shayne asked. "I thought we were moving forward. Because if we were getting even, I would've hired a hit man to take care of Russell a long time ago."

"Getting even, moving forward, call it what you want." Violet shrugged nonchalantly. "Bottom line is we're making something happen for ourselves. Not dwelling in the past. Remember that promise we made to one another?"

"I do."

"Excuse me," Fifi said, "But why are we even discussing Russell when you have a fabulous man downstairs waiting for you to show him his new home?"

"You're right." Shayne smiled as she headed toward the door. "The kids aren't home either, so now would be a good time to take him on a tour. Then by the time they get to the house, we'll feel more comfortable with one another. I decided to tell the kids that Conrad is renting a room so that I'd have extra money to help pay for Ryan's tutoring, Cadence's therapy, and the neighbor's new dog. That way, since the money will be going toward them, they wouldn't object."

"Good idea," Violet said. "Do you want to eat before you go?"

"Eat?" Shayne asked appallingly. "Are you kidding me? I wouldn't be able to keep anything down now!"

"Wow, Conrad's helping to turn your life around already!" Fifi laughed. "Vi, you've done good."

"I have, if I may say so myself."

"I concur," Shayne said, leading the way to the great room where Conrad was waiting for her.

"Hey," he said cheerily when she walked in.

"Hey. I uh . . . I'm sorry that I passed out on you earlier and missed everything. I know you probably think I'm crazy."

"Not at all." Conrad stood up and walked toward her. "Looking at things from your standpoint, I'm a perfect stranger whose background isn't squeaky clean who you're allowing into your home. That has to be a little overwhelming."

"Yeah . . . it is."

"So, shall we?"

"Sure," Shayne said even though she wasn't budging.

"Okay then, you two!" Violet headed to the door in an attempt to move them along. "I'm glad everything is working out thus far. Take care, have fun, be good, and you both know where to reach me if you need to."

"Thank you so much." Shayne hugged Violet on the way out. "We'll talk soon."

"Good luck."

Conrad reached out and embraced Violet warmly. "I can't thank you enough."

"Ditto," she replied, hugging him back.

"Good meeting you, Fifi."

"You as well. Happy trails!" Fifi waved before leaning over and whispering to Violet, "I can't believe you actually pulled this off."

"One down, two more to go," Violet responded, watching as Shayne and Conrad headed home.

# CHAPTER FOURTEEN

Violet stared out of the limousine's back window. She watched from a distance as her personal assistant Cheryl pulled her red Toyota Corolla in front of the prison. Cheryl was posing as the girlfriend of Bodie, the second inmate being released from prison. Just as they'd done with Conrad, Bodie would be given a brief description of what was going on by Cheryl before being driven down to the limo where Violet, Shayne, and Fifi awaited him.

When Bodie walked out of the gate, he saw Cheryl standing outside of the car waving at him. He approached her slowly. She embraced him and whispered something in his ear. He stepped back and smiled, then picked her up and twirled her around frantically. Cheryl laughed and pointed at her car. Bodie put her down and ran around to open her door, then he got in, and they drove off.

"Okay, here they come," Violet said, turning in her seat and looking at Fifi and Shayne. Fifi's expression was full of fear. Shayne's was full of bliss.

"Fifi, what is wrong with you?" Violet asked.

"I'm in shock."

"Why? Just look at Shayne. Her face says it all. There's no need for alarm."

"I have had more sex in the past few days than I've had in the past few years." Shayne sighed and stared off into space.

"What!" Fifi exclaimed, slapping Shayne's leg. "You didn't tell me that when I talked to you last night."

"That's because I was too busy helping Conrad with dinner. Plus, the kids were around, so I couldn't talk about it."

Fifi turned abruptly when the driver opened the door, and she grabbed her stomach as Bodie bent down and looked inside the car.

"Violet!" he yelled. "What the fuck are you doing here?"

She laughed and opened her arms. "Just get in the car, Bodie. I'll explain everything."

"Oh, God," Fifi muttered, looking over at Shayne.

"He is hot," Shayne whispered.

Bodie climbed in next to Violet and threw his arms around her. "I can't believe this! What the hell is going on?"

"You're going to have to wait until we get to my house before I can tell you anything. In the meantime, I'd like you to meet two of my dearest friends, Fifi and Shayne."

"Ladies." Bodie nodded his head then turned back to Violet. "God I'm glad to see you and not some pimp. When Meyers called me into his office, you know what I thought he wanted."

"I can imagine."

"But when he told me I was going before the parole board immediately and being released shortly thereafter, I was like, what the fuck? I thought I was being sold into slavery or something!"

"Not exactly . . ."

"So, what's up?" Bodie eyed Fifi and Shayne curiously. "At least tell me a little something. You know how impatient I am."

"I'll tell you what," Violet said, reaching into a compartment. "Why don't I pour you a glass of Blue Label, and you just relax until we get to my house for a little lunch and discussion?"

"You always did know how to settle me down." Bodie took the glass, emptied it quickly, then held it out again. "Oooh, was good. Hit me again."

"One more," Violet told him, refilling his glass. "You'll need to be in your right mind for what I have to explain to you."

"Hey, whatever it is, drunk or not, I'm sure I won't object, because it got me out of that shithole. So, cheers!" He held up his glass and grinned.

Fifi stared at Bodie through the corner of her eye, her glare filled with doubt. She then glanced over at Shayne, who appeared to be totally out of it as she stared outside obliviously. Her attention quickly turned back to Bodie when she heard him say, "But you know I wasn't trying to kill the guy!"

Violet nodded her head. "I know you weren't."

"But he just . . . he just took me there!" Bodie stared down at his hands, which were now balled into fists and shaking uncontrollably.

"Calm down, Bo," Violet said softly, placing her hand on his shoulder. "You know we've talked about this time and time again. Even though you didn't mean to kill him, you were glad that you did."

"I was, wasn't I?" Bodie's frowning mouth broke out into a huge grin.

Fifi swallowed hard and gripped the door handle, as if preparing to jump out of the moving vehicle.

"But nobody threatens somebody I care about," Bodie said, "Especially when they're about to give birth to my nephew!"

Fifi slowly let go of the handle. "Oh? So you're an uncle?"

"I am," Bodie replied proudly.

"But he almost wasn't," Violet said. "His sister's husband practically beat her to death when she was eight-and-a-half months pregnant. Luckily their neighbor called the police just in time."

"Yeah, and after I saw her laid up in that hospital with those black eyes, that busted lip, and her bruised body, I went to the house to have a little talk with her husband. But when that asshole got smart with me, that was it. I snapped."

"His neck to be exact." Violet covered her mouth while struggling not to laugh.

"I was only trying to scare him! Who knew my grip was that strong?"

"Exactly! Who knew?" Violet replied amusingly.

Fifi held her hands to her cheeks and exhaled, then leaned in toward Shayne and whispered, "The cloud of doom that had been looming over my head has suddenly been surrounded by a silver lining. Maybe this plan isn't so ridiculous after all."

"I couldn't agree more."

Bodie turned to Violet. "So come on. How and why did you get me out of jail?"

"Just be patient. You'll find out soon enough. When we get to my house, we'll sit down, have a nice Grecian salad, some risotto with rock shrimp, snow peas and mushrooms, a little tiramisu for dessert, a nice bottle of—"

"Violet got you out of jail so that you could serve as my handyman slash companion slash bodyguard of sorts," Fifi blurted out.

"Huh?" Bodie's forehead wrinkled in confusion as he looked from Fifi to Violet.

"Yep." Fifi reached for the bottle of Blue Label and poured Bodie another drink. "Those are the terms of you being released from prison."

"Fifi," Violet responded, her tone filled with shock even though she wasn't really mad. She was actually relieved that her friend appeared to have warmed up to the idea.

"Sorry for spilling the beans, Vi." There was a look of satisfaction spread across her face, to which Violet responded with a slight smirk.

"So . . . wait," Bodie said, his pupils dancing wildly. "I'm gonna be doing what?"

Violet placed her hand on his arm. "Listen, I talked to the warden and had him release you from prison so that you could help Fifi through some things she's going through in her life."

"Okay, things like . . ."

"Well, for starters, I'm pregnant. By a very important, powerful, married man who's threatening to kill me if I have the baby."

Violet leaned in toward Bodie. "He's also in the running to become the next president of the United States."

"Oh, wow." Bodie rubbed his hands over his face vigorously before sitting back and taking a deep breath.

"And Fifi is living alone in the house that her parents passed down to her after they died earlier this year. So that's only making matters worse, emotionally and otherwise."

Bodie stared at Fifi. She sat there sullenly as her expression filled with sadness.

"That is horrible," he said quietly. "What happened to your parents?"

"They died in a fire at their summer home in Malibu."

Bodie looked over at Violet, who raised her eyebrows and remained silent. "I'm so sorry to hear that. How did their house catch fire?"

"The chief was never really able to figure that out. He suspected faulty electrical wiring or something."

"What a blow."

"Yeah, it's really been difficult," Fifi whispered, blinking away tears.

"Since this guy you're pregnant by has been threatening your life, do you think he had anything to do with your parents' —"

"Oh, great! Here we are," Violet said, interrupting Bodie as they drove up her winding driveway. "Anybody hungry?"

"Not me," Shayne murmured, opening her eyes. She'd been so quiet that no one even noticed she had dozed off.

"But you have to stay for lunch," Violet told her.

"I can't. Conrad is waiting for me. We're supposed to be—"

"You're supposed to be lunching with us this afternoon," Violet said. "Conrad is just going to have to wait."

"But Bodie already knows the plan. Why do I have to—"

"Do I need to pull out your contract?"

Shayne's face fell in defeat as she slumped out of the car and walked up the stairs. "No," she said quietly.

"Good," Violet replied brightly, following her.


On the way inside the house, Fifi turned to Bodie. "So do you think you'd be interested in the plan?"

"Of course," he replied firmly, wrapping his arm around her and helping her up the stairs. "How far along are you?"

"Six months."

"Awesome. That'll give us enough time to get to know each other, get the house ready, and all that good stuff."

"Yes, it certainly will."

When they entered Violet's dining room, Bodie walked behind Fifi and pulled her chair out for her. She sat down, caught Violet's eye, and gave her a wink, appearing as though she felt well-protected already.

# Chapter Fifteen

Violet stared out of the limousine's back window. She watched from a distance as her pool boy Danny pulled his silver Camaro in front of the prison. Danny was posing as the cousin of BJ, who was the last inmate being released from prison. Just as they'd done with Conrad and Bodie, BJ would be given a brief description of what was going on by Danny before being driven down to the limo where Violet, Shayne, and Fifi awaited him.

When BJ walked out of the gate, he saw Danny sitting inside of the car throwing up a peace sign. BJ waved and approached him. Danny said something, then motioned for BJ to get in. He did, and Danny drove off.

"Okay, here they come," Violet said, turning in her seat and looking at Shayne and Fifi. Both of their expressions were full of relief. And so was hers.

"Two down, one more to go," Fifi said.

"I know," Shayne sighed. "I'm so glad this is the last time we have to do this. Conrad and I had plans that we had to cancel because—"

"Let's not forget how this whole Conrad thing came about," Violet said.

Fifi rolled her eyes. "I think she already has." Then she looked directly at Shayne. "You haven't come up for air since Conrad moved in with you. As a matter of fact, we haven't even seen or heard from you since we picked up Bodie. You could have at least called to find out how things are going with him and me."

"I'm sorry! What do you two expect? After all these years of being mistreated and deprived, I've suddenly got a man who cooks, cleans, is unbelievable in bed, tells me I'm beautiful every single day, is great with the kids—"

"Glad to hear you're all taken care of," Violet said. "Just don't forget about us."

"I haven't, and I won't."

The tense conversation ceased when the driver opened the door. BJ hopped inside the car, threw his arms around Violet, and said, "I love a woman who keeps her promise. Thank you, baby. I love you."

Violet closed her eyes and embraced him tightly. "I love you, too."

Shayne and Fifi stared at each other, their expressions filled with confusion.

BJ leaned back and took a deep breath. "I've missed you so much. It's good to be back together again, isn't it?"

"It is. It really is . . ." Violet reached inside a compartment, pulled out a bottle of Coca Cola and handed it to BJ.

"Thanks," he said, grabbing the bottle then smiling brightly. "So, you two must be Shayne and Fifi."

They both stared at him silently. After several seconds, Fifi finally spoke up. "What's going on, Violet? Did BJ already know about the plan?"

"I uh . . . n-n-no," Violet stuttered.

"Yeah, no . . . not really . . . she uh," BJ stammered.

Shayne placed her hand on her hip. "Do I need to pull out your contract?"

"No, no, of course not." Violet's eyes darted from side-to-side. "It's just that . . ."

"Violet and I go way back," BJ said. "We kinda discussed doing something along these lines back when she was still working at the prison. But I didn't know she was actually going to go through with it. I thought she was just talking."

"Come on, BJ," Violet said. "You know I don't just talk." She turned to Shayne and Fifi. "Ladies, would either of you like something to drink?"

"No," they replied in angry unison.

"All righty, then." Violet turned back to BJ. "So we're on our way to my house. We're going to have a nice lunch. Your favorite."

"You didn't."

"I did. Well, actually Rita did, but I put the menu together."

"Thanksgiving style?"

"You know it."

"Turkey, dressing, the whole nine?"

"The whole nine."

Fifi glared at Violet through eyes so piercing that they practically lit her on fire. "Too bad Shayne and I won't be there to enjoy it."

Shayne nodded her head in agreement. "Nope, we certainly won't be."

"Oh, please, Shayne," Violet said. "You're not even upset. You just want to run home so you can be with Conrad."

"I do not! And I am upset. You never told us that BJ was already in on this."

BJ held his hand up defensively. "I wasn't in on it. I swear."

Violet glanced over at BJ appreciatively. "Really, he wasn't, which is why he's going through the same routine as Conrad and Bodie. I'm going to explain all the details to him once we arrive at my house."

"As if he doesn't already know the details," Fifi mumbled underneath her breath.

"Exactly," Shayne concurred quietly.

"I heard that," Violet told them.

"Good," Fifi sassed back, folding her arms and staring out the window.

"Well, I can see we're all off to a great start here," BJ said before chuckling. Violet nudged his arm and shook her head at him. "Sorry," he told her before turning back to Shayne and Fifi. "So, how are you all's guys working out?"

"Great, just great," Shayne said.

"Ditto," Fifi replied dryly, not taking her eyes off the window.

"Yeah, you two got a couple of good guys. I was really tight with them both while we were—"

Violet quickly cleared her throat. "I've got a room set up really nicely for you." But the attempt to shut BJ up was too late.

"Oh, so he knows about our men, too?" Fifi asked. "I can't believe this!"

"Again, he doesn't know the details," Violet replied quietly.

"That's it," Shayne said, pulling out her cell phone. "You don't follow the plan, I don't follow the plan. I'm not staying for lunch. I'm going to have Conrad get dressed so we can follow through with our plans . . ."

Fifi grabbed her phone as Shayne continued rambling. "Bodie? Hey, it's me. Let's go to that baby store the decorator told us about. Yeah, I'm on my way now. No, no lunch. I'll be there in a few. Okay. Bye." Fifi disconnected the call and glared at Violet.

"So neither of you are coming to lunch?" Violet asked.

"Why should we?" Fifi responded. "Apparently that conversation was had a long time ago. So, there's no need for us to try and keep up appearances. We've met BJ, he seems to be a nice man, and we're glad your inmate made it out. Bam. What else is there?"

"Fine, then." Violet knew she was somewhat wrong for not telling her friends that she and BJ had sort of began developing her plan a while back. But it was too late to second guess herself now.

The minute the driver pulled in front of Violet's house, Shayne and Fifi jumped out of the car and stormed off without even saying goodbye.

"Nice meeting you both," BJ called out.

Shayne and Fifi waved without turning around and kept walking.

"Some thanks you get," BJ said.

"I know. Here I've helped them both turn their lives around in a matter of weeks, and that's how they treat me."

"It's okay. They're your best friends. You all will work it out."

"I know. I'll give them some time to get over it. Then I'll plan a day for the three of us to go to the spa or something. But in the meantime, we've got a lot to talk about. So let's go eat, settle you in, then bring you up to speed on the details of the plan."

# THE UPDATE

# CHAPTER SIXTEEN

Violet, Shayne, and Fifi were sitting in a private room having lunch at Victoria's Day Spa. During their seaweed wraps, aromatherapy facials, and Swedish massages, the threesome had not said a word to one another.

Shayne's cell phone rang. She frantically dug inside her purse, smudging two of her nails in the process.

"You're not supposed to have that on," Violet said.

"You're not supposed to break signed contracts," Fifi told her.

"I wasn't talking to you."

"Well, I was talking to you."

"Will you both just shut up!" Shayne snapped. "You two sound like Cadence and Ryan every morning before breakfast."

"So, what are you saying? That we sound like two heathens?" Violet asked before she broke out laughing.

"That was low," Shayne replied before giggling. "And untrue. Because lately, my children have been making me quite proud."

"Lately, huh," Violet said. "In other words, thanks to Conrad?"

"Maybe," Shayne smiled coyly.

"*Maybe*?" Fifi said, leaning back and staring at Shayne through wide eyes. "You mean definitely?"

"Okay. Fine. *Definitely*."

"Because he has certainly made a way—" Fifi started.

"Out of no way," Shayne finished before the two cackled in unison.

"Oh? And how did he do that?" Violet asked.

"I'll take this one," Fifi said. "Within the past week, Conrad has taken Matthew to the gay pride parade, tutored Ryan after Ms. Ferguson's appendix ruptured, encouraged Cadence to join a peer counseling group so that she can deal with her bulimia amongst kids her own age—"

"And do you all know that half the girls she competes against in the pageants are in that group?" Shayne whispered as if one of them might overhear her.

"And last but not least," Fifi said, "Conrad took Basil to see an anger management specialist."

"Wow." Violet folded her hands and eyed Shayne smugly. "It sounds like Conrad is everything that I told you he'd be, plus more."

"He is." Shayne smiled dreamily. "He really is."

"And what about you, Fifi?" Violet asked. "How are things going with you and Bodie?"

"They're great. He didn't get to spend much time with his sister during her pregnancy because he couldn't stand her husband, so I think he's enjoying experiencing what he missed with me. Plus, he's been running out in the middle of the night to get me peanut *M&Ms*, which I've been craving like crazy. And do you know what else I've been craving? *Meat*."

"What?" Violet gasped dramatically. "Not *you*."

"Yes me. I want a cheeseburger so badly. But I haven't given in. Not yet, at least. Anyway, back to Bodie. He's been going to my Lamaze and parenting classes with me, and ever since he started answering my phone, I haven't gotten any more of those threatening calls."

Violet chuckled. "Yeah, Edward probably thinks he's in the clear now that you've got a boyfriend."

"Have you seen that strange black *Town Car* on the block lately?" Shayne asked.

"Nope. Not since Bodie's moved in."

"So, things are working out," Violet said.

"Yes, they are. As a matter of fact, things couldn't be better."

"And as a result of me coming up with a plan that turned both of your lives around for the better, you all thank me by storming off right before BJ's lunch and not speaking to me for days on end? Just because I discussed a very small aspect of the plan with a friend before the subject even came up amongst us? I don't think that's fair."

Shayne and Fifi sat and stared at one another, then down at the floor. Shayne began picking at her lobster and crab salad. Fifi took several sips of water. Violet got up and walked away from the table.

"Wait, don't go," Shayne said to her. "We're sorry." She looked over at Fifi. When she remained silent, Shayne kicked her underneath the table.

"Sorry," Fifi finally muttered.

"Come on, Vi, sit back down," Shayne said. "We both appreciate what your plan has done for us. But while you were so stern when it came to us being discreet, signing a contract and adhering to it, we were hurt to find out you hadn't done the same."

"Yes, I had," Violet argued as she walked back over to the table and sat down. "BJ and I grew very close when he was incarcerated because he and I have a few people in common, so—"

"People in common?" Fifi retorted. "Like who?"

"I'm not at liberty to say at this time."

"*Excuse* me?"

"You'll find out soon enough," Violet told her, draining her champagne glass and getting up again.

"So first you don't tell us that BJ knows about the plan—"

"For the thousandth time, BJ did not know about the plan—"

"And now we find out you and BJ have people in common?

I don't get it. We went into this together. Because of that, I think you owe it to us to disclose who those people are and what they have to do with your plan."

"The same thing that Bodie killing his abusive sister's husband has to do with your plan," Violet said, grabbing her purse.

"Huh?" Fifi uttered. "What are you talking about?"

"Sweetie, despite what everyone seems to think of you at this point, you're a smart girl. Figure it out. Now, if you two will excuse me, I have a meeting with BJ."

"I think she's losing her mind," Fifi whispered to Shayne.

"But you haven't even told us how things are going between you and BJ," Shayne said to Violet's back.

"They're great. Ladies, I'm glad we had a chance to break the silence. Let's get together again soon!" Violet called out before leaving the room.

"Do you think they're sleeping together?" Shayne asked Fifi.

"Honey, those two are up to way more than sex."

"So you think they are?" Shayne gasped. "He's married! I didn't think Violet would do something like that."

"Have you taken a close look at Violet? She's the most beautiful woman we know. She doesn't have to go through the trouble of conning a married, mediocre-looking man like BJ out of jail just for sex."

"So, what are you saying?"

"I'm saying that Violet and BJ have something devious up their sleeves!"

"More devious than sleeping together while he's married?"

Fifi glared at Shayne for several moments before getting up. "Let's go."

"Are you mad at me too now?"

"No," Fifi told her, leading the way through the spa and out the door. "I'm not mad at you for being the sex-crazed fiend that you are."

"Speaking of which, are you and Bodie having sex?"

"Enough, Shayne." Fifi ignored the question and hugged her goodbye.

"Well, are you?"

"No! Look at me. I'm huge. Who would want me?"

"Please. I'm way bigger than you, and somebody wants me everyday day. A few times a day, I might add."

"Okay, then. Congratulations. You're having enough sex for both Violet and me. Now let me get outta here. Bodie and I are meeting with the decorator in an hour."

"Okay. I'll talk to you tomorrow!"

"Until then." Fifi waved before cramming inside her car. She rolled down the window and stuck her head out. "You know, I just may have Bodie pay BJ a little visit to find out exactly what's going on over at the Christianson estate."

"Ooh, if you do, let me know what he finds out."

"I most certainly will."

# THE CONFRONTATION

# CHAPTER SEVENTEEN

$V$iolet and BJ were sitting in her library, sifting through a pile of paperwork.

"Your wife's passport arrived much faster than I'd expected."

"Well, hey, when you've got the connections, you can make anything happen."

"So, has she seen the house yet?"

"She has." BJ smiled.

"I'm assuming she likes it?"

"She does."

"And the kids?"

"They love it."

"Great. See? I told you I'd find something wonderful. Just wait until *you* see it."

"I'm sure I'll be happy. You know you've always had the best taste."

"Why thank you," Violet said before Rita entered the room.

"Excuse me, Miss," Rita said quietly as she stared down at her fidgeting hands. "There is a visitor in the foyer who would like to see you."

"Who is it? I'm in the middle of a meeting, and I'm not expecting anyone."

"He told me not to tell you who it is and to just have you come into the foyer."

"Oh?" Violet and BJ looked at one another amusingly. "So now you're taking orders from anonymous visitors? Rita, who the hell is at the door?"

Rita teetered toward the desk, unable to look Violet in the eye. "It's Elliot's business partner, Thomas. And . . ."

"And *what*?" Violet asked as she felt her body go hot and

cold all at the same time.

"His daughter."

Violet and BJ peered at one another for several moments before she finally spoke up. "Rita, let this be the last time you ever let anyone inside this house without my permission."

"I'm sorry, Miss. I wasn't going to let him in, but he insisted, and I thought that since you knew him—"

"It doesn't matter," Violet snapped, getting up from behind her desk. "BJ, the minute I walk out of this room, lock the door, and do not come out until I tell you to."

"Yes, ma'am."

Violet strolled out of the room with Rita nipping at her heels. After she heard the library door lock, she headed down the long hallway toward the foyer. "I'll take it from here, Rita."

"Would you like for me to bring your guests something to—"

"That won't be necessary." Violet's balled up fists pressed her acrylic nails into her palms. Stinging droplets of perspiration formed along her hairline as she rounded the corner and saw Thomas and his daughter awaiting her.

"Thomas. Madison. What are you two doing here?"

"Good afternoon to you too, Mrs. Christianson." Thomas leered condescendingly. "Is there someplace we can go and talk?"

"Yes. Right here."

"Okay then," Thomas said, turning and looking down at his daughter's humungous stomach. "I'll make this quick. Madison is due any day now. It's time for you to make that move, Violet. We've held off on revealing who this child's father is for long enough. Now I don't want to make this a public spectacle. So sign Elliot's half of the business over to me, then I'll go ahead and pay the money that's owed to you from Elliot's final deals. And as an added bonus, I won't even pursue child support like I'd been threatening to do."

Violet stared at Thomas as he ran his bejeweled fingers down his pinstriped *Brioni* suit. She listened as his shiny Italian leather loafers shuffled over her marble floor. She almost laughed at the three strands of gray hair he'd combed over his shiny, balding head. Then she glanced over at Madison, who looked like a scrawny, two-dollar crack whore with her dark eyeliner and lip liner, eyebrow and lip piercings, scraggily platinum blonde extensions and denim skirt that barely covered her panties.

"Thomas, I have said it before, but I'll say it again since you appear to be a bit daft. I will not, nor will I ever, sign my husband's half of the business over to you. And rather than waste my time by coming over here asking me to, you should have added up the enormous amount of money that you owe me and slid the check inside my mail slot without bothering to ring the bell."

"Oh, Violet, come on." Thomas chuckled as he approached Madison. She moaned and shifted her weight from one leg to the other before leaning on him for support. "You know I can't do that. It wasn't part of my agreement with Elliot, may he rest in peace."

"Well, unfortunately, Elliot's no longer with us. I'm running things now. So whatever agreement you two had is null and void."

"It is? You know, Violet, I could have had a private investigator look into Elliot's mysterious death, but I didn't."

"Mysterious? He had diabetes. His blood sugar level skyrocketed, he fell into a coma and died. Where's the mystery?"

"Oh, I don't know. Maybe lying somewhere in the midst of him dying the day before he was supposed to sign his half of the business over to me."

"And here I thought you at least had a bit of intelligence.

Don't you know Elliot just told you that so he could buy himself more time? He was preparing to unleash a plan on you so treacherous that it would've taken you all the way under."

"Really?" Thomas asked, pushing Madison off of him and coming so close to Violet that she could smell his bourbon and cigar-laced breath. "Would it have taken me any further down than I was about to take him? I can't imagine it would have, considering my plan involved me revealing to our friends, colleagues, and not to mention the *authorities* that your fat, sleazy, two-timing husband impregnated my seventeen-year-old daughter. That's statutory rape, isn't it?" he turned and asked Madison.

"Yeah," Madison mumbled in between smacking bubble gum and twirling a hair extension around her bony finger.

The sound of those words made Violet's stomach turn. "Get out. Both of you," she spewed, throwing open the door.

"The police are just a phone call away, Violet," Thomas said, leading Madison out. "And so are all the people who my company —"

"You mean *our* company."

"I'm sorry. All the people who my *soon-to-be* company work with and for. Do yourself a favor. Give me what's rightfully mine before I take it from you and send you down a road of humiliating hell along the way."

"We'll see." Violet smiled pleasantly before slamming the door in Thomas' face.

She spun around and rushed to the library as fast as her spectator pumps would carry her to tell BJ all that had just transpired.

# Chapter Eighteen

"Matthew! Sloane! Ryan! Cadence! Basil! Get down here! Your father's waiting out front!" Shayne yelled for the tenth time.

"I'm so nervous," she said to Conrad while vigorously polishing her silverware. She and Conrad were preparing a lavish dinner for his parents, who Shayne was meeting for the first time that night.

"Don't be," he replied, leaning over and kissing her. "They're gonna love you. Especially if they compare you to the other women I've dated."

"I don't even wanna *hear* about the other women you've been with!" Shayne declared right before the doorbell began to ring wildly.

"Speaking of not wanting to hear about others we've been with . . ." Conrad quipped.

Shayne rolled her eyes and headed to the front door. "Will you all get down here!" she yelled toward the staircase.

The minute she opened the door, Shayne threw her hand on her hip and cocked her head to the side. "Why are you ringing the bell like a maniac?"

Russell just stood there, frozen. After several moments, he took a step back. His eyes roamed from the top of Shayne's head to the bottoms of her feet.

"What's wrong with you?" she asked.

"*You*. You look so . . . different."

Shayne looked down and ran her hand over her hair self-consciously. "Not today, Russell. I have a lot on my mind. I don't need to hear how repulsive I am."

"No! What I mean is, you look beautiful."

"I do?"

"Yeah. Look at you. You look great. And you've lost a good amount of weight."

"I have? Well, I guess since I've been so busy and happy that for once in my life I haven't been obsessing over my body."

"You're busy and happy, huh . . ." Russell entered the house and looked around. "And what have you done in here? It looks different, too. Good, but different."

"I've had a little work—" Shayne was interrupted when Conrad entered the room.

"Hi," he said, approaching Russell with his hand extended. "I'm Conrad."

Russell just stood there staring at him.

"You're Russell, right? I've heard a lot about you. Your kids are great, man."

Russell's facial expression twisted in curious frustration. "How do you know my kids?"

Shayne quickly turned to him. "This is the man I told you is renting a room."

Russell's suspicious gaze shifted from Shayne to Conrad. "Okay, you're renting a room, which means you don't have a run of the house. So why don't you go ahead and retire to your quarters, and stay away from my children."

"Russell!" Shayne gasped, placing her hand on Conrad's arm. "Why are you being so rude?"

"I'm not being rude. Just matter-of-fact. I don't like the idea of some strange man coming into my house—"

"Wait a minute now." Shayne held her hand in the air. "This isn't your house. You don't live here anymore. Remember?"

"But this is still my family," Russell argued, looking up as the children slumped down the stairs in a single file line.

"Hey, guys!" Russell threw Conrad a look before approaching the kids. "I've missed you all! How is

96

everybody?"

"Fine," they replied dryly, wilting like dying flowers in Russell's arms as he hugged them tightly and showered them with kisses. Their reaction was lackluster. Their reciprocation was nonexistent.

"You all ready to go?" he asked them excitedly. "I've got a great weekend planned for us."

"I don't wanna go!" Basil whined, running over to Shayne and throwing his arms around her. "Mommy, you and Conrad promised to take me to the action figure convention this weekend!" he whimpered.

"I know, sweetie. But that was before your father called wanting to see you. So go ahead. We'll make it up to you."

"You will?" Basil asked through teary eyes.

"They extended the convention through next weekend, buddy," Conrad told him, rumpling his hair. "So we'll go then."

"Promise?"

"Promise."

"What about me?" Matthew asked Shayne and Conrad. "You all were supposed to go to the school rally this weekend and talk to the principal about the prom."

"And you all promised to take me shopping for a dress for Paige's super sweet sixteen party," Sloane cried.

"Conrad, you said you'd help me with my history paper that's due Monday," Ryan told him.

"Who's gonna go to counseling with me?" Cadence asked Conrad wearily.

Shayne and Conrad looked from the children to Russell sheepishly. Awkwardness filled the air. Silence fell over the room until Russell opened his mouth.

"What the fuck is going on here?" he yelled. "Who the fuck *are* you?" he asked Conrad. "Are you fucking my wife?"

Shayne's mouth fell open. She grabbed her children by the

shoulders and pushed them toward the stairs. "Kids, go to your rooms. *Now!*"

"Does this mean we can go to the convention?" Basil asked her.

"We'll talk about it later."

"Bye, dad!" the children yelled excitedly as they ran upstairs.

Conrad crossed his arms and turned to Russell. "How could you talk to your kids like that?" he asked.

"If you know what's good for you, you'll refrain from speaking to me and retreat to your room so that I can talk to my wife."

"I am not your wife. Have you forgotten that we're divorced?"

"Well, this is still my house because I believe I'm still paying the mortgage on it. So please ask your boarder to leave the room so that I can speak to you privately."

"No," Shayne said, walking toward the front door. "What I'm going to do instead is ask you to leave. And as for the mortgage, if not paying it will prevent you from ever walking in here and acting this way again, then stop. It's a new day, Russell. We're not married anymore. You will never speak to me the way you used to again. Now," she continued, opening the door, "goodbye."

"What the hell has gotten into you?" Russell asked on his way out.

"Love," Shayne said before slamming the door in his face and running into Conrad's arms.

"You were great," Conrad told her as the kids came flying back downstairs, screaming and clapping their hands.

"Mom! That was awesome!" Matthew said. "Dad totally deserved that shit, too."

Shayne laughed while pointing at him. "Watch your mouth."

"So, does this mean we can go to the convention?" Basil asked again.

"Yes," Shayne replied, "We can go to the convention."

"Yay!" Basil screamed, jumping up and down.

Shayne turned to Conrad. "But what about your parents? Is it okay if the kids stay for dinner?"

"With them here, it'll be even better."

"Thank you," Shayne whispered. Her eyes filled with tears. "I'm gonna go check on the duck," she sniffed, rushing to the kitchen so that no one would mistake her tears for anything but joy.

# CHAPTER NINETEEN

"Did you find the rake?" Fifi asked Bodie as she kneeled on her front lawn and planted another tulip in the ground.

"I did. It wasn't in the basement, though. It was in the—"

"Bodie? Bodie Jacobs?" Fifi heard behind her. She turned around abruptly. And there, stepping out of a black *Lincoln Navigator*, was Senator Edward Hynes.

"Edward!" Fifi said, jumping up as fast as she could and rushing over toward him. "What are you doing here?"

"I came to speak with Mr. Jacobs."

"I'm sorry," Bodie said, approaching them, "Do I know you?"

"No, you don't. Senator Hynes," he said, extending his hand.

"Bodie Jacobs. What can I do for you?"

"Can we go inside and talk?" Edward asked Fifi.

"Sure," Fifi replied nervously, wondering how Edward knew Bodie.

Fifi led them into the living room and offered Edward a seat. "Can I get you anything?"

"No, no, I won't be long." He set a metal briefcase down on the coffee table and unlocked it. "Go ahead and have a seat, Fifi."

Bodie stared down at the floor, his brows furrowed and leg shaking nervously. Fifi sat down next to him and placed her hand on his knee, bracing herself for the bomb that Edward was undoubtedly about to drop.

"So, how are we doing today?" Edward asked in his best campaign-speech voice.

"Fine," Fifi responded while Bodie remained silent. She

could feel angry heat coming from his body.

"Great, great." Edward pulled a file from his briefcase and tossed it onto the table. "Well, I'm here today to discuss this . . . *situation* that we're in."

"What about it?" Bodie shot back.

Edward stared at Bodie for a few moments, seemingly taken aback by his tone. "Forward and aggressive," he said. "I like that. I'd offer you a job if you weren't a convicted murderer." Edward opened the file then looked up at Bodie. "So, how'd you do it?"

Fifi swallowed hard, her entire body stiffening up.

"Do what?" Bodie asked, his voice rising.

"How did you get out of jail?"

"I'm out on parole."

"Oh? Because according to these records I've got sitting here in front of me, you were serving a life sentence and weren't eligible for parole for another twenty-five years."

Bodie looked over at Fifi. She looked back at him, then over at Edward. "Your records must be incorrect. According to the state prison's files, Bodie was up for parole this year."

Edward burst out laughing. "Do you think I'm stupid? I have access to records that go way beyond the state prison's."

"Why don't you call the warden and ask him about it?"

"Why talk to Gordon when I can talk to the man who signs Gordon's checks? And maybe you should tell Gordon that the next time he pulls a stunt like this, he should be sure to have every single record in the state changed."

"What do you want, Edward?" Fifi asked in an effort to avoid incriminating herself or anyone else.

"Ahh, I'm glad you asked." Edward stood up and paced the floor. "See, I don't have a problem with you pulling a few illegal strings to get your boyfriend out of jail."

"He's not my boy—" Fifi said. But Edward spoke over her obliviously.

"I wouldn't be where I am today if I hadn't pulled a few strings myself. Thing is, there's a price to pay for every illicit favor you request. And yours, my friend," he said, pointing down at Fifi's stomach, "Is ceasing your little child support campaign, aborting a baby that has no place in this world, and apologizing to my family and colleagues for mistakenly believing that you were pregnant with my child."

Bodie jumped out of his seat and grabbed Edward by the collar. He held him so forcefully that Edward's feet were barely touching the floor. "Get the fuck outta here," Bodie spat in his face.

"You ready to go back to prison already?" Edward laughed, pushing Bodie off of him and straightening his blazer. "Here I am, giving you an opportunity to stay out, and you're just dying to go back. I guess you're one of those who can't function in normal society."

"Come on," Fifi said, pulling Bodie away from Edward. "He's not worth it."

"Make your life easy, Fifi," Edward told her, sliding the file back inside his briefcase and heading toward the door, "Before you end it."

Bodie tried to punch Edward in the jaw when he walked past him, but Edward ducked just in time.

"Just let him go," Fifi said.

Edward shook his head and laughed, then walked out.

"Are you okay?" Bodie asked Fifi as tears poured from her eyes.

"No!" Fifi screamed, charging into the den. "I've got to call Violet so she can find out what the hell is going on!"

# THE REVISION

# CHAPTER TWENTY

Violet, Shayne, and Fifi were sitting in Violet's sunroom. Violet, who looked somewhat alien-like as a result of the Botox injections she'd endured that morning, was patting ice over the lumps that were strewn across her forehead. The cool cubes, along with a glass of vodka tonic and chain of cigarettes, were helping to ease the pain.

Shayne, who looked to have lost thirty pounds or so, was sipping a glass of water. And Fifi, who looked to have gained a good thirty pounds or so, was eating a two-pound bag of peanut *M&Ms*.

"What have we gotten ourselves into?" Fifi asked, staring off into space and shaking her head. "Edward's got us by the balls."

"No, he doesn't," Violet said. "No man could ever sabotage a woman to the point where he'd have her by the balls. That's why we don't have any."

Shayne cackled loudly. "I like that."

"I would too if it were true," Fifi told them.

"How does Edward have us by the balls, Fifi?" Violet asked.

"Because he knows that I had something to do with Bodie's records being changed. And if he does enough probing, he'll find out about BJ and Conrad, too. Then if he does enough interrogating, he'll find out exactly how and why they were released from prison early."

"The warden was instructed to change every record across the board. He has enough pull to make that happen, and believe me, with what I've got on him, he will."

"I really need to know the details of this bribe, Violet. Because if they're not strong enough to keep things under wraps, then Edward could dig deeper, figure this all out and take us all down."

"I'll put it this way," Violet said. "You know how some sick, homosexual priests hide behind the church in order to take advantage of vulnerable boys? Well, some sick, homosexual prison officials hide behind the criminal justice system in order to take advantage of vulnerable inmates."

"So, you're saying that the warden is involved in some sort of sexual activity with the prisoners?"

"Nonconsensual sexual activity."

Shayne gasped sharply. "So they're actually *raping* the prisoners?"

"Amongst other disgusting things."

"Oh my," Shayne said, looking over at Fifi and gripping her chest. "Sounds like the warden will do all that he can to keep this under wraps."

"He may, but Edward will find another way to—"

"Fifi," Violet interrupted exasperatedly, "What exactly did Edward say when he came over?"

"First he said he knew I'd pulled some strings to get Bodie out of prison early. Then he said I'd better stop my child support letter-writing campaign, have an abortion, and apologize to his family and colleagues for accusing him of getting me pregnant."

"Or else?"

"Or else he'd have Bodie thrown back in prison and kill me."

"Oh, my goodness," Shayne moaned.

"This is horrible," Violet added, laying her pounding head in her hand. "Why would you even want to have that man's baby?"

"Because I did love him at one point," Fifi responded quietly, holding her stomach. "And even though I don't anymore, I have certainly grown attached to our child. I'm not going to get rid of this baby."

"You know I would never ask you to do that," Violet said, reaching over and rubbing Fifi's belly.

"So what am I gonna do?"

"What if you and Bodie just run off?" Shayne said. "Just disappear so that you can have your baby and live safely and peacefully?"

"I'm not leaving my house. I've wanted nothing more than to raise this child in the same home where my parents raised me."

"Then, you're going to have to lie," Violet said before draining her glass and standing up. "For starters, do not send Edward another child support request letter. Instead, send him a letter stating that in exchange for his silence, you've aborted the baby—"

Shayne threw her hands in the air. "But that's impossible!" Look how far along she is."

"It's possible," Violet told her. "It's called a late termination of pregnancy, and the procedure spans over the course of two days. Now Fifi, after you send that letter, write one to his wife and everyone at his office telling them that you were lying about being pregnant. Tell them you were just obsessing over Edward, to the point where you temporarily lost your mind and made yourself believe that you were pregnant."

"Are you seriously asking me to do all that?"

"Are you seriously willing to risk your life as well as the life of your child's by *not* doing all that? What's more important, your pride or your existence?"

"My existence," Fifi mumbled. "*Our* existence."

"Exactly. So do what you have to do to get your baby here, and once that's done, we'll go from there. Now Shayne, what's going on with you?"

"My life is great," she said, nibbling on a grape.

"Somewhat amusing, but great."

"Oh? How's that?" Violet asked before calling Rita and requesting another drink.

"The last time Russell came over to pick up the kids, he was telling me how great I look and mentioned how much weight I've lost."

"Which you have," Violet said while Fifi nodded her head in agreement.

"Why thank you, ladies. Russell also met Conrad, and he was *extremely* rude toward him. He kept asking who Conrad is, calling me his wife and saying that the house is his. It was crazy. I've never seen him act like that before."

Violet shook her head and laughed. "Can you say, *regret*?"

"Yeah, sounds like he found his way out of that asexual abyss that you'd supposedly sent him into," Fifi said.

"Apparently so. Because he's sent me three bouquets of flowers this week apologizing for leaving me. And he's called several times asking if he could take me out to dinner. It got so bad that I had to tell him to stop calling me altogether and to just call the kids on their cell phones if he needs to reach them."

"What does Conrad have to say about all this?" Violet asked.

"He acts like it doesn't bother him. But I think it does."

"I'm sure it does," Fifi said. "How was dinner with his parents?"

"Wonderful. They fell in love with the kids, who weren't even supposed to be there. But that was the day Russell came over acting crazy, so they ended up staying home. I'm glad they did, because they definitely helped to lighten the mood. And they were so well-behaved. By the end of the night, Conrad's parents were asking if he and I were thinking about marriage."

"So, you two are moving right along," Violet said. "What

are you going to do about Russell?"

"Ignore him. After the way he treated me, he doesn't deserve an ounce of my attention."

"Amen," Fifi said. "See? I like where your head's at. But be careful. We don't want Russell's curiosity and jealousy to backfire on us."

"Because he definitely wants you back," Violet said. "And if he sees that you don't want him because of Conrad, who knows what he may try and pull or find out."

"So just be on the lookout," Fifi told her before turning to Violet. "What about you and BJ? How are you two doing?"

"Not good. Not good at all."

"Why not?" Shayne asked. "Was he a bad choice for you? See, I knew you shouldn't have gotten someone who was married."

"That has nothing to do with it. Elliot's business partner Thomas and his daughter came by the other day."

"Oh no," Fifi groaned. "What did they want?"

"For me to sign over Elliot's half of the business."

"Why would you do that?" Shayne asked.

"I wouldn't. But they think that by trying to bribe me, I would."

Shayne held her hands to her face. "Bribe you? How?"

Violet glanced at Shayne, then Fifi. Their eyes were filled with such sincere concern. She took a deep breath, debating whether or not she should tell them the truth. They'd been so painfully honest with her. So after a few moments, Violet decided to come clean.

"Thomas' daughter, who you both know is pregnant with Elliot's child, is . . . seventeen-years-old."

"Violet!" Shayne and Fifi screamed simultaneously. "She's *what*?"

"Seventeen," Violet repeated before yelling, "*Rita*! Bring me an unopened bottle of *Chopin*!" Then she turned back to her friends. "No need for the service bell when you've got pipes like that," she added in an attempt to lighten the mood.

"Violet, we had no idea that Thomas' daughter was so young," Fifi said.

"I know. It's disgusting, isn't it? I was so embarrassed I couldn't even say the words until just now."

"Do your business associates know the baby is Elliot's?" Shayne asked.

"No, and I'd like to keep it that way. But Thomas is threatening to tell everyone and ruin the Christianson name if I don't sign over my half of the company."

"That's ridiculous," Fifi said as Rita scurried in with Violet's bottle of vodka. "I know you're not going to do it."

"Of course not. You know me. I wouldn't be who I am if I hadn't already come up with a plan for the plan."

Shayne turned to Violet as her expression filled with confusion. "Huh?"

"Didn't I tell you she and BJ were up to something?" Fifi told Shayne.

"How do you know?" Violet asked.

"Because . . ." Fifi hesitated before taking a deep breath, then continuing, "I just figured you'd be using a guy like BJ for something beyond a boy toy."

"And you were right. I'm going to have BJ secure a job at Thomas' estate so that he can see what he and Madison are really up to."

"Okay, I see where you're going with this," Fifi said.

"Yeah, you never know. By the time I'm done with him, I may be walking away with Thomas' half of the business."

"You wouldn't have it any other way," Shayne said.

"I certainly wouldn't. Ladies, shall we carry this into the dining room and continue over lunch?"

"Certainly," Fifi said, getting up. "I'm starving."

"I guess I could have a bite," Shayne told her.

Violet grabbed her bottle, glass, and cigarette case, and headed to the dining room. She wondered why she hadn't trusted her friends enough to tell them the whole truth before. But then she remembered. The less they knew, the better.

# THE EXECUTION II

# CHAPTER TWENTY-ONE

"I got the job!" BJ exclaimed the minute he walked through the front door. He'd just returned from Thomas' house, where he'd gone to interview for a position as manager of the groundskeepers.

"Wonderful!" Violet clapped her hands and hugged him tightly. "I knew you'd pull it off. When do you start?"

"Monday. But get this. While Thomas and I were sitting in his study negotiating my salary, Madison walked in whining about how her computer had just crashed. Thomas went off and told her to get out because he was in the middle of something, and she just fell out crying. So I asked him if I could take a look at the computer just to get her out of the room. I did, and Thomas was so impressed that he asked if I wanted to be his computer consultant."

"You're kidding."

"I wouldn't kid you on this. Do you know what that means?"

"Indeed I do," she said, this news so delicious that it made her mouth water.

Violet spun around on her heels and sauntered down the hallway, her mind already going in a thousand different directions. "Have Rita send in a couple of *Sapphires* on the rocks and a Coke for you, and meet me in the library."

"Will do."

Violet sat down behind her desk and pulled out the files on the latest deals that Thomas had yet to pay her for. When BJ walked in, she looked up at him and smiled. "I'm so in love with what you accomplished today that I could kiss you."

"Now, now." BJ laughed and sat down across from her. "You know Fiona wouldn't appreciate that."

Rita scurried into the room and sat the drinks down on the desk. "Are you ready for lunch, ma'am?"

"No, this'll be it for me," Violet said, sitting back and lighting a cigarette. "BJ?"

"No, I'm good. I grabbed a sandwich after the interview."

"Okay, then. That'll be all for now, Rita." Violet took a sip of her drink and turned to BJ. "This is going to be so much easier than I could have ever imagined."

"Oh, you have no idea."

"Here are the files that contain information on the final deals that Elliot worked on with Thomas," Violet said, sliding the stack of folders across the desk. "Since you'll now have access to Thomas' records, I want to start by finding out exactly how much money he owes me. Elliot was so sick before he passed that his records weren't being maintained and updated properly. I don't even know if and when half of these deals actually did close."

"Come on, Vi. You know Elliot never met a deal he didn't close."

"That's true. You know, I always told Elliot that he was too nice. Sometimes stupid even. There's no telling how much money Thomas swindled from him, even when he was in good health. Elliot was never one to dot his i's and cross his t's. The only thing he ever cared about was securing a deal and collecting his money. He let Thomas handle everything else. I always got on him about that, but all he wanted me to do was stay quiet and shop. I could spend the money, but I couldn't see to it that Elliot was being paid correctly."

"That's because you were Elliot's trophy," BJ said solemnly. "He didn't respect your intellect."

"He didn't, did he? Even though I have more education than he did. But unlike him, I didn't grow up in the streets. Elliot thought his *school of hard knocks* degree was superior to any accreditation that he could have gotten from a university."

"He did. Too bad that so-called degree didn't teach him ruthlessness like it did Thomas."

"Oh, Elliot was ruthless," Violet said, side-eyeing BJ knowingly. "But only in his personal life. He was a fool when it came to business. And me wanting to help him made him feel like less of a man. As if it wasn't my place to get involved in his affairs."

"Well, we're about to fix all that, aren't we?"

"We most certainly are. By the time we're done with Thomas, he'll be handing over every single dime I'm owed, plus more than he ever bargained for."

"Alls he had to do was give you what's rightfully yours. But now?" BJ shrugged. "For all your pain and suffering? He's gotta pay out the ass."

"And too bad his daughter has to be involved in this, but oh well, she shouldn't have been fucking my husband," Violet said, draining her glass then grabbing the other drink. "Let's go ahead and figure out what's missing in these files, then decide what your tactic will be once you've pulled Thomas' records."

"Sounds good." BJ pulled his chair closer and grabbed the folder at the top of the pile.

# CHAPTER TWENTY-TWO

"He's here *already*?" Sloane whined to Shayne when she heard the doorbell ring. "I'm not ready to go! Chuck is supposed to be calling me about tonight's basketball game."

"He should just call your cell phone," Shayne said.

"But he doesn't have the number! Ashley was supposed to get it from Jenny and give it to him, but she never did!"

"Well, if Chuck calls while you're gone, I'll just give him your cell number myself. Okay?"

"Chuck isn't that class president you were caught in the theater with, is he?" Conrad asked as he rubbed Shayne's shoulders.

"No! We haven't spoken since the day you went up to the school and had that little chat with him."

"Good," Conrad replied firmly.

"Why don't you go get the door," Shayne told Sloane after Russell rang the bell for a third time.

"You go!" Sloane bounced up the stairs. "I have to get my bag."

"Tell your brothers and sister to get down here while you're up there!" Shayne yelled at her back. She turned to Conrad and rolled her eyes. "Why don't you go check on the chicken?" she said before going to the door.

"The chicken is fine. It won't be done for another thirty minutes. And I know what you're trying to do."

"Then go do it," she said as the bell rang for the fourth time. "I'm not in the mood for another confrontation."

"Yes, ma'am," Conrad barked, saluting Shayne jokingly then marching out of the room.

As soon as he was gone, Shayne threw open the door. "Sorry I kept you —"

"Hello beautiful," Russell said, handing her a bouquet of flowers.

"Hi. What's this?"

"Just a little something from me to you."

"But why? You never even bought me flowers when we were married."

"Things change. And people change," Russell said, placing the bouquet into her hand and walking into the house. "So, where's your *boyfriend*?"

"If you're referring to Conrad, he's in the kitchen."

"Look, I need to talk to you. Can we go upstairs?"

"Upstairs?"

"Not to the bedroom, Shayne. Let's go into the television room. I need to talk to you in private."

"Fine." Shayne could feel Russell's eyes all over her as she spun around and headed up the stairs. She walked down the hallway and knocked on all the kids' doors, saying, "Your dad's here. Everybody downstairs in five minutes."

"*Ugh*," she heard coming from each of their rooms.

"Glad to know I've got such big fans in my own children. "What have you been saying about me?"

"Do I have to say anything?" When they entered the television room, Russell shut the door. Shayne turned to him and crossed her arms. "So, what do you need to talk to me about?"

"Shayne, you know I still love you, don't you?" he asked, trying to take her hands in his. She stepped away and remained silent. He dropped his head and continued. "I just . . . I'm just trying to figure out what this Conrad thing is all about."

"Why?"

"Because he's living in my house, he's developing close relationships with my children—"

"Russell, this no longer your house. You keep forgetting

that you don't live here anymore. And I'm allowed to let another man into my life, aren't I? Because we are divorced, aren't we?"

"Yeah," Russell said after a long pause. "But what's with him and the kids? He's all they talk about. It's as if he's taken my place."

"Whose fault is that?"

Russell stared at Shayne through pained eyes. "Where did you meet him? What does he do? Where's he from? Why is he renting a room in this house rather than living in his own home? When—"

"Why are you asking all these questions? What business is it of yours?"

"It's certainly my business when he's spending so much time with my children. So I have a right to know his background."

When he stepped in closer and peered at Shayne, her frustration turned to panic. Russell had numerous acquaintances in the judicial system and relationships with countless attorneys. It wouldn't take him long to exhume Conrad's criminal background if he chose to go on an excavation.

"Well?" Russell asked.

"I met Conrad through Violet," Shayne blurted out. And then her heart began to palpitate because she might have already said too much.

"Violet?" Russell's eyebrows shot up toward his hairline.

"Yes."

"How does Violet know him?"

Shayne bent over and pretended that she'd just been overcome by a fit of coughs.

"Did he work for her or something?"

Shayne's coughing suddenly ceased. She stood up slowly. "Yeah . . . he worked for her."

"On what? A new construction?"

"Exactly." Shayne smirked, wondering why she hadn't come up with that herself. "He helped build a few of Violet's new constructions."

"Okay," Russell said slowly. "So why is he staying here and not in his own home?"

"Because his girlfriend recently passed away, so he wanted to get out of the apartment they were living in immediately since the memories were just too much for him. And I'd mentioned to Violet that I wanted to rent a room to help with extra expenses. So, she told Conrad, and he moved in."

"When is he leaving?"

"I have no idea. Since the money he's paying me every month is going to good use, I'm hoping no time soon."

"If you needed money, why didn't you just come to me?"

"Russell, I don't want anything from you. Your only obligation is to take care of the children. Beyond that, I can take care of myself."

"Fine," he replied.

Shayne heard the sound of feet flying down the stairs. "The kids are waiting for you," she told him, opening the door. "Why don't you go ahead and start your weekend. I'm sure everybody is looking forward to spending time with you."

"Yeah, right." Russell waved her off and slumped out of the room.

Shayne sighed with relief and fanned her damp face, following behind him.

"Hey, guys!" Russell said, bouncing down the stairs with open arms.

"Hi," the children replied dryly.

"Everybody ready? I've got a great weekend planned for us."

"Whoohoo," Matthew muttered, twirling his finger in the air cynically.

"Mom, don't forget to give Chuck my number when he calls, okay?" Sloane asked.

"I won't." Shayne doled out kisses to everyone. When Russell reached out to her, she ignored him and walked over to the door.

"Where's Conrad?" Basil asked. "I wanna say goodbye. I won't get to see him again 'til Sunday night!"

Shayne looked at Russell hesitantly. He shook his head and turned to the kids. "I'll just wait for you all in the car," he told them before ducking out the door.

"Conrad!" the kids called out the minute Russell was gone. "We're leaving!"

Conrad jogged out of the kitchen and laughed as the children wrapped him up in a big embrace.

"We don't wanna go," Cadence whined into Conrad's chest.

"Don't worry," he told them. "The weekend will be over before you know it."

"We wish it was over now," Matthew said.

"Okay now, you all go ahead," Shayne said. "Don't leave your father waiting." She hugged and kissed everyone goodbye again, and once they were gone, turned to Conrad wearily. "Russell asked me a hundred questions about you."

"And I'm sure you answered them all very eloquently," he told her, laying her head against his chest and holding her tightly.

"Not really. He caught me off guard asking where you came from and how I met you and what you do. Violet and Fifi warned me that he may try and dig up some dirt on you because they think he wants me back, but I think I handled the situation."

"What did you tell him?" Conrad asked, pulling away and looking at her through concerned eyes.

"I told him that I met you through Violet, and after that, he asked me a slew of other questions that I just said yes to. So, he thinks you worked on Violet's new constructions and that you're living here because you had to leave the apartment you shared with your deceased girlfriend."

"Okay." Conrad sighed as he ran his hand over his hair. "Do you think he bought it?"

"I do, actually. But you know, of all the things that could go wrong with this plan, I never once thought Russell would be a possible factor. He left his family because he found me repulsive and our children embarrassing. So why does he care who I'm with now?"

"Because he realizes how big of a mistake he made," Conrad said softly, taking Shayne's hand and leading her into the kitchen. "And seeing another man make his family happy is making him sick. But let's not worry about it. You did just fine in telling him who I am. We're going to stop thinking about Russell, sit down and enjoy our dinner, and spend the rest of the weekend alone in the house making love."

"That sounds wonderful," Shayne murmured, turning off the stove while Conrad grabbed the plates.

"I love you," he told her.

Shayne stopped in the midst of pulling the chicken from the oven. Heat blasted her face and turned her cheeks even redder than Conrad's statement just had. She turned around and faced him. "What did you say?"

"I said, I love you."

Shayne covered her face as tears rolled down her hands. "I love you, too," she whispered, her voice muffled behind her palms.

"Come on now, don't cry." Conrad took the chicken out of the oven then removed her hands from her face. "Let's eat."

"Afterwards," she purred before turning around and leading him upstairs.

# CHAPTER TWENTY-THREE

"I did it," Fifi said to Violet when she answered the phone. "Good. Was it hard?"

"Extremely. To the point where every word I typed in those letters brought on labor pains. It got so bad that Bodie had to take me outside to get some air."

"Is everything okay?" Violet asked anxiously. "You didn't start spotting, did you?"

"No, no, nothing like that. Everything's fine."

"Thank God. You could've miscarried over this."

"And that would have defeated the whole purpose. Just imagine how much Edward would have loved that."

"I know. So, keep that in mind next time you start stressing and getting upset. The only two people you'd be hurting are you and the baby."

"You're right. I just still can't believe I actually did this."

"What, lie?"

"I don't feel like I just lied. I feel like I compromised my integrity. I'm an activist at heart. I stand up for people's rights. So naturally, I feel strongly about my right to have this child. Everyone else should, too. So why sell myself out and appear to be a crazed, delusional stalker by saying that I was never pregnant, all for the sake of Edward?"

"Fifi, this is not about integrity, nor is it about Edward's sake. This is about survival. You're being threatened by a very powerful, ruthless man who goes after what he wants at whatever cost. He's made it clear that nothing is off limits. Including the lives of you and your child."

"But no matter what, writing these letters proclaiming that I'm a liar just so that Edward's reputation can remain intact just sickens me. His wife and colleagues need to know who he really is. And if a man who would threaten the life of his own child becomes the president of this country, God help us."

"I know, Fifi," Violet said sympathetically. "But just think of it as self-preservation. These letters are a means to an end. If you use your resources properly, that end could certainly be to your satisfaction."

"What do you mean?"

"Figure it out, sweetie. So, have you sent the letters off yet?"

"Bodie did. He actually had to finish writing them for me because after we came back inside, I just couldn't bring myself to sit down at that desk again and type one more word. I'm telling you, Vi, Bodie has been so good to me. I'm almost in my eighth month, and this would have been the roughest time for me if it weren't for him."

"All this is coming from the woman who was most resistant to the plan."

"I know. But hey, I tried it my way, it didn't work, and I was big enough to admit that and come crawling back to you. At least give me credit for being humble enough to do that."

Violet giggled. "I give you all the credit in the world for doing that. Plus, you know I didn't want to go through this alone."

"I figured you didn't. And that's exactly what I told Shayne. That poor woman thought she'd actually missed the inmate release deadline."

"As if I would have actually imposed a deadline on my two best friends. I must be one helluva bluffer."

"Indeed, you are," Fifi said before her tone turned serious. "Look, I have another concern."

"What is it?"

"I'm afraid that Edward is not going to believe me when I tell him I had an abortion. He knows how determined I am to have this baby. What if he wants proof?"

"Have you checked your fax machine?" Violet asked.

"No. Why?"

"Just go check it."

Fifi wiggled her way off the couch and headed upstairs to her office. When she reached the machine, she saw that a fax had come through.

"Did you get it?"

"I got something," Fifi replied as she grabbed the paper. It was an invoice from the Choices Medical Center that had her name on it and was dated seven days prior to today's date. The bill stated that she'd received a general anesthesia abortion. "Violet, how did you do this?"

"Come on, now. I got three convicts released from prison. This was nothing."

"You never cease to amaze me."

"Hey, I just do what I have to in order to protect those I love."

"Thank you, Violet."

"Don't mention it. Now hurry up and fax it over to Edward's office so that you can get him off your back. I don't want to hear anything else about you cramping or stressing. The remainder of your pregnancy needs to be as peaceful as possible, because I'm so looking forward to meeting your baby."

"It will be. And I'll let you know if Edward responds to this fax or my letters."

"I'm sure he will. And when he does, he'll undoubtedly express nothing but gloat-filled gratitude. Is that Bodie I hear in the background?" Violet asked.

"Yeah, he just got back. I need to go get dressed. He's taking me out for a relaxing dinner."

"Nice. Well, have a good time. And don't forget to keep me posted."

"I won't. Love you."
"Love you, too."

# THE LEGITIMIZATION

# CHAPTER TWENTY-FOUR

Violet sat down at the head of her dining room table and looked around at her guests. To her left was Shayne, looking stunning in a short black lace *Prada* frock, and Conrad, dapper in a custom black suit and crisp white shirt.

To Violet's right was Fifi, glowing in a silk floor length saffron dress, and Bodie, handsome in a gray cashmere sweater and tailored slacks. And across from Violet was BJ, sitting tall in the brand-new navy-blue suit and pale blue shirt she'd bought for him that morning.

But Violet was the fairest of them all in her flowing floral *Ungaro* gown. She had invited her friends over for an elaborate celebratory dinner of sorts. But tonight was about more than just toasting with a blanc de blanc and socializing over seared scallops, fresh greens, lobster bisque, French rack of lamb, and vanilla bean crème brulee.

This plan of Violet's had garnered a little more attention than she'd anticipated. Unforeseen questions were being asked. Unanticipated threats were being made. So before any unauthorized information fully surfaced, Violet wanted to sit down with her comrades under pleasant circumstances and discuss their next move.

"I'd like to first thank everyone for coming," Violet said as Rita walked around the table pouring wine in everyone's glasses.

"Thank you for having us." Shayne smiled, gazing at the elaborate tropical floral centerpiece and antique hand-painted place settings that surrounded it. "Everything looks so beautiful."

Fifi nodded her head in agreement while sipping herbal tea. "Yes, Vi, it really does."

Violet waited until Rita was done serving the appetizers before raising her glass. "Let's start by making a toast. To the continued success of the plan. May the end result be as valuable and effective and as it has thus far."

"*More* effective," BJ said before winking at Violet.

"Yes. More effective."

"Hear, Hear," everyone chimed in, clinking, then sipping from their glasses.

"Bon appétit," Violet said.

Fifi took a bite of food and chewed slowly. "Mmm, this is delicious," she said, referring to the organic roasted vegetable platter Rita had prepared especially for her.

"So is this," Conrad said as he fed Shayne a scallop.

"I'm glad you're enjoying it." Violet glanced over at BJ while he eyed her. For the next twenty minutes, they performed a visual dance until Rita served the main course. That was when Violet nodded at BJ, and he asked for everyone's attention.

"I've got some great news," he said.

"Oh yeah?" Bodie asked in between bites. "What's that?"

"I'm sure all of you know by now that I've been working for Elliot's ex-business partner, Thomas."

"We heard," Shayne said. "Nice move."

"And it's only getting nicer. I've been able to get into some of Thomas' records, and so far, I've discovered that he owes Violet well over three million dollars. And that's only from a few of the deals that he and Elliot worked on together. So imagine how much more he owes."

"Are you *serious*?" Shayne asked, looking from BJ to Violet.

"Absolutely," BJ replied. "So I'm making a list, checking it twice, noting that Thomas is nowhere near nice."

"*The criminal needs to get out . . . of town*," Violet sang to the tune of "*Santa Clause Is Coming To Town*" before everyone broke out into laughter.

"But seriously," Fifi said, "How are you going to get your money?"

"Well, you've got to know that if Thomas did this to Elliot, he's been doing it to plenty of other people. So BJ's going to infiltrate his computer system until we have all the information we need in order to get everything we want."

"And what is it that you ultimately want?" Bodie asked.

"Ultimately? More than Thomas could ever imagine giving up."

"So, Conrad," BJ quickly interjected after Violet threw him a look, "I hear you're having a pretty good time over at the Wentworth house."

"Oh, I'm having a great time," he responded, leaning over and kissing Shayne.

"How have things been between you and Russell?" Violet asked him.

"Strained, to say the least. We thought he was okay after last weekend when he interrogated Shayne half to death. But then he called Tuesday night insisting that she go to dinner with him."

"And Conrad made me go!" Shayne said.

"Just to keep him and his questions and suspicions at bay, sweetheart," Conrad said softly, as he rubbed her back.

"Wait, you actually went to dinner with Russell?" Fifi asked.

"Unfortunately. And it was hell. That dinner didn't keep anything at bay. Once again, he kept questioning me about Conrad and how he just popped up out of nowhere. He even commented on how Conrad is always lurking around the house and wants to know how he's paying me rent if he's not working."

"What did you tell him?" BJ asked.

"That he must spend his money wisely."

Conrad nodded in agreement. "And I'm in between jobs

while waiting on Violet's next real estate deal to close."

"Do you think he might resort to using his own resources to find out more?" Violet asked.

Shayne sighed and reached for Conrad's hand. "I hope not."

"Well, Conrad," Violet said, "I think it's time for us to legitimize you."

"Legitimize me?"

"Yes. Legitimize you. Russell is watching. His newfound interest in Shayne could get complicated. If he does enough inquiring amongst his colleagues, he could learn of your record. And I'd hate to see what he'd do with that information."

Shayne dropped her fork and clutched her pearl necklace. "What if he takes me to court and tries to get custody of the kids?"

"Hold on, now, let's not panic," Violet responded. "Things are not going to go that far. Because I've got an idea."

"Good." Shayne exhaled. "What is it?"

"Before Elliot died, he and I had been talking about starting up a construction company. Then he passed, and I just didn't have the energy to move forward on the idea. But I'm in a different place now, and I've got BJ here to help me. So I'm going to proceed in making it happen. And Conrad, I'd like for you to head it up."

"Really?" Conrad asked, his face lighting up.

"Violet!" Shayne clapped her hands vigorously. "That is a great idea!"

"Good. And that way, Russell will see that Conrad is legit. He'll be up and out every day, working and earning money."

"Does your ex know that you and Conrad are involved?" BJ asked Shayne before looking at Violet. She winked at him, appreciative of his stepping in so that she wouldn't appear too pushy.

"No," Shayne and Conrad replied simultaneously.

"Are you sure?" Violet asked. "You all don't think the kids said anything?"

"The children don't like talking to Russell, so they keep all conversation with him at a minimum. Plus, they know he isn't fond of Conrad, so that makes them clam up on the subject even further."

"He does ask about me though," Conrad said. "The kids have told me that he's constantly pumping them for information. But they don't give him anything."

"Good," Violet said.

"Vi, maybe you should go to the women's correctional facility and have a female inmate paroled for Russell so that he'll stop obsessing over Shayne," Fifi said.

Violet laughed and slapped her hand against the table. "Oh, I think I've done enough." She turned to Fifi and Bodie. "So, what about you two? Anymore trouble from Edward?"

"Not since we sent the letters and I faxed him that faux invoice from the clinic," Fifi replied.

"Any black *Town Car* sightings?"

"Every now and then," Bodie said. "But not to the point where we feel threatened."

"I think we need to consider legitimizing you as well, Bodie," Violet told him.

"But Edward already knows my deal."

"I know. I just want things to appear as normal as possible. You popped up out of nowhere. Our nosy neighbors are probably wondering where you came from but are afraid to ask Fifi. That doesn't mean they won't talk amongst themselves and try and figure it out. Plus, if Edward has people keeping an eye out, it would be a good look for you to be functioning as a normal member of society."

"That would be cool," Bodie said. "But what would I do?"

"Well, you're an architectural engineer, so I'm sure we can

find a place for you. Ideally, you'd be working for my real estate business, but since that's temporarily on hold, you can work with Conrad at the construction company. Then once BJ helps me get everything squared away with Thomas, which won't take long at the rate he's going, you can start doing things on the development end."

"That sounds like a great idea," Fifi said to Violet before turning to Bodie. "What do you think?"

"Works for me. I miss putting my skills to good use," Bodie said before turning to Fifi. "Not that I haven't been enjoying everything I've done for you."

"Thank you." Fifi smiled and patted Bodie's shoulder while everyone looked on endearingly.

Rita and her assistant maid walked in and began clearing the table. "Are you ready for dessert, ma'am?" she asked Violet.

"Yes. But none for me. I'll just have a gin on the rocks."

"Yes, ma'am."

"This was scrumptious," Shayne said, dabbing the corners of her mouth with her napkin. "Thank you again, Violet."

"It was, yes, thank you," everyone echoed.

"We should do this again soon," Conrad said. "Same time tomorrow?"

"Hey, why not," Violet laughed as Rita rushed back in with dessert.

While her guests ooh'd and aah'd over the crème brulee, Violet discreetly glanced at BJ. He gave her an inconspicuous thumbs up. She subtly raised her glass then took a sip of gin. They were both relieved that everyone had taken to her ideas. Because Violet could not afford for her plan to go wrong. After all, of the three of them, she'd stuck her neck out the farthest to see the scheme through. And if anything went wrong, she would certainly be the one who'd lose the most.

# THE ARRIVALS

# CHAPTER TWENTY-FIVE

"It's a girl."

The words nearly knocked Violet out of her hairstylist's chair. She pressed her cell phone against her ear. "What? When?"

"Early this morning," BJ replied.

"Is she . . . is she okay?" Violet choked.

"She's fine. Beautiful. Eight pounds, ten ounces."

"You saw her?"

"I did. Thomas was still at the house this morning when I got there—"

"Why wasn't he at the hospital with Madison?" Violet shrieked.

"According to him, he had too much work to do. So he just sent her off with the driver and the baby's nanny."

"Thomas is just vile," Violet spat.

"I know. I made him feel so horrible for not going with Madison that he eventually asked me to take him to the hospital. That worked out perfectly, since I wanted to see the baby and report back to you anyway."

"Good job," Violet said, her heart thumping at an abnormal rate.

"And do you know that I ended up spending more time with Madison and the baby than he did? He could've just stayed home considering the way he worked on his laptop in the waiting area the whole time."

"Figures. So what did she name the baby?"

"Britney Ciara. After two of her favorite pop stars."

"Once again, figures," Violet said before looking up at her stylist. "Are you almost done?" she asked him.

"I've got one more extension to install, then you'll be all

set. Are you getting your lashes done today, too?"

"I don't have time," Violet responded before turning her attention back to her call. "Where are you now, BJ?"

"On my way back to Thomas' house. Everybody's still at the hospital, so I'm going to use this time to see what I can find."

"Excellent idea. I'm going to go home and see if the equipment arrived. If it hasn't, I'll just pick it up from the store."

"Sounds good. I thought we'd have at least another week to get organized."

"So did I. But now we need to move as quickly as possible. How are we going to get everything set up in time?" Violet asked, her tone filling with anxiety.

"Come on, Vi. Don't forget who you're talking to here. I can make anything happen. So, no need to panic. I'll have everything up and running before Madison even comes home from the hospital."

"And what will be your explanation for lurking around her room?"

"I'm uploading photos of the baby onto her computer so that she can email them to her friends."

"And you'll have enough time to do that and get set up without looking suspicious?"

"Absolutely."

"I'll take your word for it." Violet jumped up, tipping her stylist and air kissing him goodbye.

"I haven't let you down so far."

"And now is not the time to start."

"I won't," BJ said assuredly. "I'm pulling up to Thomas' house now. I'll give you an update on everything when I get home tonight. And Vi?"

"Yes?"

"Stay calm. You've come too far to start getting nervous

now. You already pulled off the bribe of a lifetime, because Conrad, Bodie, and I are free men. We went on to bring your vision for you, Shayne, and Fifi to life. So be cool. You're going to get everything you want and deserve, plus a whole lot more."

"Thank you, BJ," Violet said quietly. "I'm so glad I've got you."

"Same here. Now let me go get started before Thomas comes home."

"Okay. I'll talk to you soon."

Violet hung up the phone and almost knocked the valet over as she shoved her ticket in his hand. Then she jumped in her car, hit the accelerator, and prayed that the surveillance system she'd ordered had been delivered.

# CHAPTER TWENTY-SIX

"It's a boy."

The words nearly knocked Violet off of her chaise lounge. "What? When?"

"Late this afternoon," Bodie replied.

"Are they . . . are they okay?" she choked.

"They're fine. Fifi's resting now. And he's beautiful. Six pounds, twelve ounces."

"Oh, good." Violet sighed, patting her chest then turning to BJ. "Fifi had the baby. They're both fine."

He gave Violet a thumbs-up then turned his attention back to the video camera in his hand.

"What did she name him?" Violet asked Bodie.

"Lance. After her father."

"Sweet," Violet replied softly, wishing Fifi's parents were still here so they could meet their grandchild. "Were there any complications since she delivered early?"

"Her blood pressure was a little higher than normal, but other than that, no."

"I'm not surprised, considering how stressed she's been. All her worrying probably forced the baby out early."

"More than that, she knew Edward and his cronies were going to be campaigning in the area over the next several days, so I think her body subconsciously went into labor," Bodie said.

"Of course. She didn't want to run the risk of being seen."

"Exactly. Fifi's no fool."

"Well, hey, she pulled it off. She's fine, the baby's fine, and Edward won't know anything about this," Violet declared.

"God willing. I'm gonna go back in and check on Fifi and the baby. Can you call Shayne for me?"

"Of course. When is Fifi going to be released?"

"Probably the day after tomorrow. The doctor wants to make sure her blood pressure stabilizes."

"Okay. Well, tell her we love her and that we'll come and see her tomorrow."

"Sure thing."

Violet hung up the phone and pulled the last tiny microphone from a box. "Is everything here?" she asked BJ.

"Everything's here."

"Wonderful. Now let's go over the set up one last time. You're going to install cameras and mics in Madison's bedroom and bathroom, the baby's bedroom, and Thomas' bedroom and office, right?"

"Right."

"And you'll install Madison's while she's at school, baby Britney's while she and the nanny are at the doctor, and Thomas' while he's at his office in the city."

"Right."

"And you think you can get all of this done tomorrow?"

"I *know* I can get all of this done tomorrow."

"Okay," Violet said, her hands shaking as she began placing the equipment inside five separate bags, one for each room being staked out.

"Vi."

"What?"

"Stop it."

"Stop what?"

"Getting nervous."

"I'm not nervous!" Violet said, cursing herself for doing exactly what she was known for never doing — losing her cool.

BJ kneeled down and helped Violet pack the rest of the bags. When she got up and began pacing the floor, he said, "Tell you what. Let's go downstairs, have Rita fix you a nice cocktail, me some dinner, then we'll go into the theater room and watch *The Thomas Crown Affair*. That should make you feel better."

"All right," Violet replied before sighing heavily and running her damp palms over her red silk kimono. "But it probably won't."

"Well, let's give it a try," BJ said, wrapping his arm around her.

Violet leaned her head against his chest as they headed toward the door. "If this plan doesn't work, your ass is going back into the clinker."

"I know!" BJ laughed. "That's exactly why I'm going to see to it that it does."

# THE DEPARTURE

# CHAPTER TWENTY-SEVEN

"A n ex-*con*, Shayne?" Russell yelled.

"What?" Shayne choked, so shaken by Russell's words that she had to turn around and walk away from him.

"Get back here!" he screamed, lunging forward and grabbing her arm. "You owe me an explanation!"

It was Monday morning, and Shayne had the whole house to herself for the first time in months. The kids were at school, and it was Conrad's first day at Violet's construction company. The mood had been so cheery before everyone left, and Shayne was extremely happy. She'd finally felt as though her life was coming together. Her children had straightened up and were doing better than ever, she had a man in her life who loved her as much as she loved him, and she was looking and feeling as beautiful as she did back in her pageantry days.

But then, after everybody was gone and Shayne began clearing the breakfast dishes, the doorbell rang. She thought it was the UPS man delivering her new treadmill, elliptical machine, and Pilates apparatus she'd ordered. When she swung open the door, however, it was Russell, standing with a sweaty face and heaving chest. Before she could say a word, he shoved her to the side and stormed inside the house.

Russell gripped Shayne's arms and pulled her in so close that his mouth pressed firmly against her ear. "I want that man out of here *immediately*."

"What is wrong with you?" Shayne squealed, pulling back and wincing at the crazed look in his dilated eyes.

"You're jeopardizing the lives of my children."

"What are you talking about?"

"Conrad Tate, the man who you allowed into this house without my approval and let fraternize with my children, was convicted of murder in the first degree."

"No, he wasn't!" Shayne cried, struggling to push Russell off of her.

"Call the law firm. Ask Joel."

"You have pulled a lot of stunts, but this one is by far the worst yet."

"I'm telling you the truth, Shayne. Conrad is a convicted killer. And I want him out of this house. *Right* now."

"No."

"This is not up for debate."

"Russell, I want *you* out of this house. Right now," Shayne said before spinning on her heels and marching back into the kitchen.

"If I walk out of here without your word that you'll get rid of Conrad immediately, I will go straight to the police, then to the courthouse to file for full custody of our children."

Shayne stopped dead in her tracks and turned back around slowly. "On what grounds?"

"On the grounds that you've got a convicted felon living here in the house, whether he's a killer or not."

"Well, if he isn't a killer then he wouldn't pose a threat to our children."

"He will once I plead my case to Judge Steele, my law school mentor and close friend who I'd arrange to have preside over the case," Russell said before a sinister smile spread across his face.

"Why are you doing this?" Shayne uttered, squinting her eyes and walking toward Russell slowly. "Why do you even care? The main reason you left this family was because you were so embarrassed by your kids. Why would you want to take them away from me?"

"I don't necessarily want to take them away from you. I'd love to see our children remain in this house with their mother."

"So, you just want me to get rid of Conrad."

"That, amongst other things . . ." Russell said before his voice trailed off.

"What other things?"

"Oh, I don't know. Like uh," Russell began arrogantly, shoving his hands in his pockets and rocking back on his heels, "I move back in."

"*No!*" Shayne said, shaking her head firmly. "You are not moving back into this house. You left here under the most cruel and unusual circumstances while we all begged and pleaded with you to stay. And you think you can just come back now that we're all happy and settled in our new lives? Absolutely not."

"Why don't I give you a day to think about it," Russell said, walking toward the door. "But you don't have much choice. It's either get rid of Conrad and I come back home, or you lose the children *and* him."

"I hate you," Shayne choked, watching him leave through teary eyes.

"Don't worry. You'll learn to love me again," Russell replied hauntingly before walking out the door and closing it softly behind him.

# CHAPTER TWENTY-EIGHT

"He has to go," Violet said, freshening her manicure with a coat of clear polish.

"I agree," Fifi said as she breastfed Lance. "He does have to go."

"But why?" Shayne whined, pacing back and forth between the two of them. Both Violet and Fifi had rushed over to Shayne's house after she called, crying hysterically after Russell's threats. "I don't believe Russell's going to do anything. He's just bluffing. He doesn't want our children."

"Shayne, you humiliated him," Fifi told her. "He never expected you to move another man into the house that he'd just left, let alone fall in love with him."

"And don't think for one second Russell can't tell you and Conrad are involved," Violet said.

Fifi nodded her head. "Oh, anyone can see that. Plus, Conrad's got a relationship with the children that Russell could only dream of having. And look at you!"

"You look better than ever," Violet said. "So, of course he wants to come back home."

"Do you all understand what Russell has put me through?" Shayne wailed. "I do not want him back in my house! I'm in love with Conrad, the children are in love with Conrad, and *he's* the one we want."

"And he's the one you all will have . . . eventually," Violet said. "You know I'll see to that. But for now, you need to lay low so that Russell won't stir up any trouble. I've spoken with the warden since Edward threatened Fifi with those unedited records he supposedly got a hold of, and Gordon promised me he'd look into it and have them changed immediately."

"But even still," Fifi said, patting Lance's back until he

burped loudly, "You don't want the courts getting involved in this. After what we've done, we don't need any additional heat on us."

Violet stared at Shayne while blowing her nails dry. "We absolutely don't need any extra heat on us."

Shayne flopped down onto the couch. "So, you all want me to put Conrad out and let Russell come back?"

"It sounds so harsh when you put it that way," Fifi said.

"It does," Violet said softly. "But yes, Conrad is going to have to leave for a while, and Russell's going to have to come back home, just until we figure something out."

"I would've been better off not even going through with the plan."

"Now why would you say that?" Fifi asked.

"Because it's backfired in my face. I would've rather not gone through this at all than have something so great given to me then snatched away. Especially if in the end I was going to have to take Russell back."

"Shayne, you can't actually believe that," Violet said. "You've gotten more out of this than you ever could've imagined. And again, this change is only temporary. You'll get your life back. Trust me."

"But where is Conrad gonna go? And I hope you all don't expect me to sleep with Russell."

"Conrad can stay with me," Violet told her. "And no, we absolutely do not expect you to sleep with Russell."

"I wouldn't even allow him in the same room as me," Fifi said. "Let his ass stay in the bedroom that he thinks Conrad lives in."

"Good idea," Violet said. "And you're more than welcome to come to my house and see Conrad whenever you'd like."

"Thank you," Shayne muttered. "But we'd better come up with an alternative plan fast. Because I don't know how long I can live under such horrific conditions."

"We will," Violet said, reaching over and squeezing her arm. "I'm proud of you for even being willing to live under such horrific conditions. I know this isn't easy for you. But keep in mind it's only temporary. You're a strong woman, Shayne. And I think that's something you've taken for granted about yourself."

Fifi looked over at Shayne and nodded her head. "I totally agree with Vi. But since this newfound happiness has come into your life, you're more confident than ever. And that's probably what Conrad loves and what your kids have come to respect about you."

"You two are really pouring it on thick, aren't you?" Shayne said, her frown slowly transforming into a slight smile.

"We're telling you the truth!" Violet said.

"Yeah, right. You all just don't want me to turn Russell down and run the risk of having all of us thrown in jail!"

"She's got a point there," Fifi told Violet.

Violet waved her off before turning to Shayne. "Are you going to talk to Conrad when he comes home tonight?"

"I guess . . . I just can't believe this is even happening."

"Keep in mind, it's only temporarily," Fifi said as she got up and grabbed her bag.

"When is Russell trying to move back in?" Violet asked.

"From the sound of things, tomorrow."

"So he's not wasting any time," Fifi said.

"And neither am I," Shayne replied. "I do not want that sorry excuse for a man and a father back in my life for long. So Violet, get to planning."

"Why don't I start by contacting one of my private detective friends, just to see what Russell has been up to?"

"That sounds like a great idea," Fifi said. "Because any man who claims to be asexual after fathering five children has got to be up to something."

"Very true," Shayne said, sitting up abruptly. "When can you call him?"

"Her." Violet blew her nails one last time before standing up. "I'll go home and call right now."

"Ooh good. When do you think she'll get started?"

"For what I'm willing to pay for your happiness, immediately," Violet responded, reaching out and hugging Shayne tightly.

"You're the best, Vi."

"I do what I can," she told her before turning to Fifi. "Can I walk you home and help get Lance settled?"

"That would be great, since Bodie's off *working*," Fifi said jokingly, throwing Violet a look.

"Hey, if Shayne can put Conrad out and let Russell move back in for the time being, you can deal with not having Bodie at home for a few hours a day."

"I guess . . ." Fifi handed Violet her baby bag while she carried Lance. "Shayne, let us know how things go."

"I will. Thanks so much for coming over and helping me through all this, ladies," Shayne said, blowing air kisses then walking them out.

Once they were gone, Shayne slumped up the stairs to her bedroom and threw herself down onto the bed, wondering how in the hell she would break the horrendous news to Conrad that night.

# CHAPTER TWENTY-NINE

"Shayne? Hun?" Russell called out.

"*What!*" Shayne barked, storming into the television room for the fourth time in the past half hour.

"Can you bring me another beer?" Russell was laid out on the couch dressed in a plaid bathrobe and sweat socks, gorging himself on smoked sausage, beef jerky, chili cheese dip, and nacho chips. A college football game was blaring from the television, which had Russell yelling out a slew of obscenities every few minutes.

Shayne snatched three empty beer bottles off the table and glared at him disgustedly before stomping back out of the room. Russell had only been back in the house for a week, but he'd managed to irk both her and the children to no end. Apparently, he'd developed a plethora of nasty habits while living on his own, the worst being laziness and gluttony.

When he wasn't at work, Russell was at the house either sprawled out on the couch watching tv, eating, or sleeping. He hadn't been spending any quality time with the kids, not that they cared. And he'd slyly sneak out of the guest room and slip into bed with Shayne practically every night, begging her for sex until she beat him back out the door.

Not only was Russell's behavior repulsive, but his appearance was as well. He'd packed on a good thirty pounds and appeared completely unkempt. Stress had caused his normally thick, wavy hair to thin in the front, and fat bags to form underneath his pinched eyes. A poor diet consisting of fast food and fattening snacks had turned his typically clear complexion spotty and chiseled face chubby. The patchy beard he'd grown in an attempt to camouflage some of the damage had only worsened his ragged exterior.

Shayne cringed on the way to the kitchen. Going from seeing a handsome man like Conrad every day to a slug like her ex-husband was nothing short of pure hell. And the way the kids had cried when they found out Conrad was leaving and Russell was coming back was excruciating. But it was nothing compared to the way Conrad reacted when Shayne told him the news.

As soon as he walked through the door after his first day of work, Conrad's delighted expression turned to worry when he laid eyes on Shayne. She'd been standing by the door waiting for him, her eyes damp and head hung low. She burst into tears the minute he asked what was wrong and sobbed into his shoulder while he held her. But it was Shayne who ended up having to do most of the consoling once she told Conrad the reason she was crying.

While Conrad initially claimed he understood why Shayne was doing this, he seemed livid when he stormed into his room and began shoving clothes inside a suitcase. He continuously yelled out that he couldn't believe he was being put out so Russell could come back home. And no matter how many times Shayne pleaded her case, he kept reiterating his shock and disbelief.

But the most heartbreaking moment occurred when Conrad was leaving. He'd turned to Shayne and said, "If I would have known this was going to happen, I would've rather stayed in prison." Now, as she stood at the kitchen window watching Conrad, Violet, and BJ laughing on Violet's front lawn, Shayne was overcome with bitter loneliness. The kids had visited Conrad almost every day since he'd moved out, but she hadn't seen him at all thanks to Russell's never-ending demands. At first, Shayne just blew off his constant requests, but once he began using the same threats he'd alluded to in order to get back in the house, she quickly succumbed.

While Shayne stared longingly at Conrad, he turned around and looked over at her house. Their eyes met, and just when he held his hand up and waved, Russell called out Shayne's name.

"Damnit!" she yelled, running upstairs and practically throwing the bottle of beer at him.

"Thanks, babe," he muttered, never taking his eyes off of the television.

Shayne rushed back out of the room, deciding that she'd go over to Violet's to see Conrad while Russell was preoccupied. But by the time she flung open the front door and stepped onto the porch, Conrad, Violet, and BJ were speeding off in Violet's black *Jaguar*.

Shayne waved her arms wildly trying to get their attention, but it was too late. She watched them turn the corner, then slowly sauntered back inside the house. The minute she closed the door behind her, Russell started up again.

"Darling!" he hollered. "Can I get another round of sausage? A little hotter this time? With barbeque sauce on the side?"

Shayne dragged herself back into the kitchen, now feeling totally defeated. She grabbed her phone and called Violet's cell. When she didn't answer, Shayne left a voicemail message saying that she needed an emergency update from the private investigator. Because if something wasn't uncovered soon, she just might end up in jail for first-degree murder.

# THE THING OF NAUGHT

# Chapter Thirty

"I got nothing."

Violet tapped her pale cream manicured nails on the arm of her chair and stared at BJ from across her desk in disbelief. "Excuse me? What do you mean?"

"I mean," BJ repeated, his voice a little shakier this time as he pulled audiotapes and a logbook out of his bag, "I got nothing."

"How is that possible?" Violet asked, her voice rising. "You've been recording throughout Thomas' house for weeks!"

"I know. But nothing seems to be going on over there. You can look at and listen to the footage for yourself. But I'm telling you. There's nada."

Violet sat back in her chair and glared down at the tapes and logbook. She opened the book and read a couple of entries, which were dated by the week. One said *Morgan's Bedroom – Audio*. The other said *Thomas' Office – Video*. And next to them both was *No Relevant Data Collected*.

Violet threw the book across the desk and moaned frustratingly. Then she grabbed her glass and knocked back a healthy dose of vodka. Before she was able to slam it back down onto the desk, BJ was pouring her a refill. And as soon as she reached for her cigarette case, BJ began fumbling around in his pocket for a lighter. The minute Violet slid a cigarette between her fingers, he reached out and lit it.

"It's only been a few weeks, Vi," he said softly, struggled to steady his trembling hand. "Give it some time."

"Time is the one thing that I don't have," Violet replied, inhaling deeply and exhaling a heavy puff of smoke in BJ's face. "What about Thomas' records? Have you found anything there?"

"No." BJ choked on the thick white fumes, discreetly waving his hand in front of his face.

"Wait, you're telling me that all you've managed to accomplish thus far is uncovering how much more money Thomas owes me from a few of Elliot's final deals?"

"Well . . . yeah, but uh . . . isn't that good? He owes you over five million dollars!"

"So what?" Violet said before quickly draining her glass. BJ went to refill it, but she held her hand up. "That means nothing to me. Thomas and I are in a race to the finish line, and right now it looks like he's going to win. If he does, not only will I never get that money, but I'll lose my half of the business, my integrity, and my credibility. As you know, I do not lose. So I need for you to comb through those files word for word until you come up with something. And keep those cameras and audio recorders rolling twenty-four-seven. Because if nothing surfaces . . ."

"It will." BJ opened a bottle of water and quickly downed it. When the doorbell rang, he jumped up and practically ran out of the room. "I'll get it!" he panted.

Violet sat motionlessly and stared at the wall. Things were not going as planned. And she did not like it when things didn't go as planned. Violet had promised herself after miscarrying her baby that she would never lose control of a situation ever again. This situation would be no exception.

When she heard footsteps charging down the hallway, Violet looked toward the door and saw Shayne rush into the room.

"Violet!" she screamed. "Russell tried to rape me!"

"*What?*" Violet jumped up and hurried over to her. The left sleeve on Shayne's lilac silk blouse had been torn, and her black pants were unbuttoned and halfway unzipped. "Oh, no," Violet moaned, reaching out and hugging her, "What happened?"

"I was in the bathroom getting dressed when the phone rang. I heard Russell walking down the hallway, so I ran into the bedroom to grab it before he could. But he beat me to it, and whoever was on the other end hung up when Russell answered. Of course he insisted that it was Conrad and tried to trace the call back to him. But whoever it was blocked their number, so Russell couldn't find out who it was. At that point, it didn't matter anyway. He was convinced it was Conrad."

"I'm sure it wasn't him," Violet said, putting her arm around Shayne and leading her over to a chair. "Conrad knows to stay far away from you and Russell. I've told him that we're handling things and that I don't want him getting involved."

"Are you positive? Because ever since Russell has moved back in, we've been getting a lot of hang-ups."

"I seriously doubt that it's Conrad. But just to make sure, why don't I have the private investigator come over there while Russell's at work and put a tracer on the phone?"

"That would be good. At least then I'll know who it is."

"Maybe it's one of the kids' friends," Violet said.

"The kids don't even get calls on the landline. All their friends call them on their cell phones."

"Well, I'll have Susan hook that tracer up as soon as possible. Now, are you okay? Can I have Rita get you anything?"

"A glass of wine would be nice."

Violet walked over to the intercom and hit the speaker button. "Rita, can you please bring two glasses of red wine into the library?"

"Yes, ma'am."

Violet slowly sat down next to Shayne. "Can you tell me what happened when Russell tried to attack you?"

"Well," Shayne said, folding her arms tightly, "After

realizing that he couldn't trace the call, Russell threw the phone across the room and pushed me down onto the bed. He said he's sick of being relegated to roommate status and wants to be treated like my husband again. I tried to get up, but he grabbed my arms and shoved me back down, hence the rip in the blouse. I kicked him, and that's when he grabbed my leg and pulled me toward him, tearing at my pants until they came undone. So, I kicked him again, and that time, I was more successful with my aim. He grabbed his balls and rolled over onto the floor, and I came running over here."

"At least you got away from him," Violet said right before Rita brought in their drinks.

"Thank you." Shayne grabbed her glass and took a long sip of wine, unaware of Rita's roaming eyes observing her frazzled clothing.

"That will be all," Violet said firmly, her tone indicating that Rita needed to mind her business and get the hell out of the room.

"Yes, ma'am," Rita said before she fingered Shayne's sleeve and shook her head.

"Rita!" Violet snapped. "That will be all!"

She threw her hands up apologetically, then shuffled out of the room.

"She's just concerned, bless her heart," Shayne said.

"She's just nosy."

"So, what are we going to do about Russell?" Shayne asked. "Have you heard anything from the private investigator?"

"Not yet. But she's on it. She'll call me as soon as she finds something."

"I don't know how much longer I can live like this," Shayne whimpered.

"Yeah, same here." Violet picked up her glass of wine and taking several sips.

"What do you mean?"

"BJ has been watching Thomas and his daughter, trying to catch them in some sort of compromising positions, but so far he's come up with nothing. And I don't know how much longer I can hold off Thomas. Soon he's going to tell everybody about Elliot and his daughter, which would ostracize me from the real estate business for good. Either that or I'll have to give in and hand over my half of the business, and in turn, lose the millions of dollars that Thomas owes me. Either way, it's a no-win situation."

Shayne threw her hands in the air. "This is terrible. Nothing is going as planned. We're all worse off than we were before the plan even went into effect."

"Not really," Violet said before draining her glass and standing up. "We've made some progress. Look at you. You've practically transformed into a new person, your children are doing better than ever, and you've found real love. Fifi delivered a healthy baby and has an unbelievable supporter in Bodie. And I've got my own little mole planted right inside of Thomas' house."

"That's all well and good, but I'm tired of being patient. I want some results. Some action!"

Violet felt a rare expression of sympathy covering her face. "It's only a matter of time, Shayne. We just have to be patient. That private investigator is going to come up with something on Russell before you know it, Edward's plan to punish Fifi and run this country is going to crumble, and the surveillance equipment that BJ has set up all over Thomas' house is going to pick up something incriminating. It's inevitable. Life always has a way of catching up to horrible people, and Russell, Edward, and Thomas are no exception."

"You think so?" Shayne asked, her high-pitch tone filled with hope.

"I know so. You mark my words. We're going to walk

away from this with more than we ever dreamed of gaining. Just you wait and see."

"Thank you, Violet!" Shayne exclaimed, jumping up and throwing her arms around her.

"You're welcome. Now, why don't you go on upstairs and say hello to Conrad? You haven't seen him since he's moved out."

"He's here?" Shayne asked excitedly. "I thought he'd be at work!"

"Not yet. He's going into the office a little later this afternoon. So go on. I'm sure BJ has told him that you're here by now anyway."

"Yay," Shayne cheered gleefully, clapping her hands as she skipped out the door.

Violet smiled and watched her leave, glad that the combination of her pep talk and Conrad had put Russell right out of her mind. But as she heard Shayne bounce up the stairs, Violet wondered whether or not she believed a word she'd just spoken.

# THE ATTEMPT

# Chapter Thirty-One

"So it's official," Violet said to Shayne the minute she picked up the phone.

"What's official?"

"You haven't heard? Turn to CNN. They just announced that Edward made it onto the presidential ballot."

"He *did*?" Shayne gasped. "So, he's actually running?"

"Apparently so."

"Oh, my goodness," Shayne said quietly. "Poor Fifi. What did she say when you told her?"

"I haven't talked to her yet. When I called the house, she wasn't there. I guess she and Bodie are taking advantage of the fact that Edward's still out of town campaigning and actually went out."

"I wonder if she's heard the news yet."

"Probably not."

"Did you try her cell?" Shayne asked.

"No, I didn't want to bother her. If she's out having a good time, let her enjoy herself and hear about this later."

"What is she going to do? This could be dangerous. You know Edward isn't going to take his presidential run lightly. So, if he finds out she didn't really . . ." Shayne's voice trailed off.

"Well, he hasn't found out so far." Violet flipped through the news channels and saw Edward's face on every one of them. "But now that he's running for president, I think it's time for Fifi and Bodie to enter my witness protection program. I could set them up so that they'd never be found."

"But you know she's not going to do that. Fifi is determined to be free, stay in that house, and raise her child her way. Plus, she would never leave her work."

"I know." Violet sighed. "But after what he did to her parents . . ."

"Yeah. I'm scared."

"I am, too. Oh, hold on. I've got another call coming in." Violet switched over to the other line. "Hello?"

"Violet!" Bodie hollered.

"Bo, calm down. I already heard the news. How did Fifi take it? Is she okay?"

"No! She's not!"

"But didn't she see this coming? Edward's been campaigning his way onto that ballad for quite some time now, and—"

"Violet!" Bodie yelled. "Fifi just got hit by a car!"

"Wait. What?"

*"Fifi just got hit by a car!"*

Violet jumped up and quickly shoved her feet inside of her shoes. "Bodie, where are you?"

"St. Joseph's Hospital. Can you come down here?"

"I'm on my way. Is Fifi all right?"

"I don't know," Bodie cried. "She looks pretty messed up."

"Where's the baby?"

"Right here with me."

"So, Lance is okay?"

"Yeah, he's fine. Fifi hadn't taken him out of the car yet when somebody drove past and hit her, and—"

"Hold on, Bodie. Let me hurry up and get there, and you can give me all the details then. Okay?"

"Okay. *Hurry.*"

"I will." Violet switched over to the other line. "Shayne, get dressed. Fifi got hit by a car, and she's in the hospital."

"Oh, my God! Was she hurt?"

"I don't know. We'll find out when we get there."

"Where is my jacket?" Shayne said as Russell called her name. "Oh, no. I forgot I told Russell I would—"

"*Fuck* Russell!" Violet screamed. "I'll be in front of your house in five minutes."

Violet disconnected the call and flew down the stairs two at a time before rushing out the door.

Violet and Shayne entered Fifi's hospital room quietly. Bodie was sitting over in the corner with tears streaming down his face and Lance lying in his lap.

When she heard Shayne slap her hand over her mouth and sob loudly, Violet looked over at the bed. Fifi was lying there with both of her blackened eyes swollen shut. Her bruised cheeks and busted lips were red and puffy. Clumps of bloody hair were stuck to her scalp and forehead. Violet closed her eyes as she felt Shayne drop her head onto her back.

"She's asleep," Bodie whispered.

Violet nodded and tightened her lips, determined not to let one tear fall from her eyes. It was enough that Shayne was breaking down all over her, and Bodie was crying in the corner. One of them had to keep it together.

Violet wrapped her arm around Shayne and led her over to Bodie. They sat down across from him, and Violet grabbed his hand and squeezed it tightly. "So what happened?"

Bodie sniffled before wiping his face and staring up at the ceiling. "We'd just gotten home from the museum, and I had gone to open the front door while Fifi got the baby out of the car. I parked on the street, since we were gonna run right back out to the grocery store after Fifi changed Lance's diaper. When she got out, she went to get Lance, and as soon as she opened the door, a black *Town Car* came tearing down the street and just . . . just *hit* her."

"Did you see who was driving the car?" Violet asked as Shayne looked over toward the bed then turned back around and wept into her shoulder.

"No. The windows were tinted."

"Well, we already know who's behind this," Shayne said in between sobs.

"Yes," Violet said quietly. "We do."

"How are we going to handle this, Violet?" Shayne asked abruptly. "I thought your plan was supposed to prevent something like this from happening! I thought your agenda was going to keep Russell out of my life and a good man in it! Not to mention get you your money from Thomas and maintain your half of the business!"

"Shh, calm down Shayne," Violet said sternly.

"No, *you* calm down," Shayne spewed before getting up.

Violet looked over at the bed and saw Fifi beginning to stir. "Shayne, please, sit back down." She grabbed her hand. "Come on. We'll get this all figured out."

Shayne snatched her hand out of Violet's grip. "No, we won't. I thought you knew what you were doing. I thought we could trust you. I thought this elaborate plan of yours was going to turn our lives around for the better. But now, everything's all fucked up!"

"Can we please focus on Fifi right now and be thankful that she's alive, and worry about where the plan went wrong later?"

"No! I wanna focus on where the plan went wrong *now*!"

Violet rolled her eyes at Shayne, then turned to Bodie. "Does Fifi have any internal injuries? Or bleeding?"

"Luckily, no. Her collarbone and right leg are broken, and her ribs are bruised. The doctor said that she looks much worse than she is. You know Fifi's too stubborn to suffer any serious injuries."

Violet giggled softly. "That's so true."

Shayne turned to her abruptly. "How could you laugh at a time like this?" she shrieked.

When Violet heard Fifi moan and saw her touching her face, she grabbed Shayne's arm and pushed her out of the room. The minute the door closed behind them, Violet let her have it.

"You selfish *bitch*. All you really care about it getting Conrad back in that house, isn't it?"

"All I care about is the fact that my best friend failed me. Failed *us*."

"This isn't over yet, Shayne."

"Oh, no? Well, let's see now. Your private investigator? Nothing. Your surveillance cameras? Nothing. Fifi's letters and fake abortion invoice? Nothing."

"But you did fall in love, didn't you? And BJ is still in Thomas' house doing all that he can to get what I need, isn't he? And Fifi held Edward off long enough to have her baby, didn't she?"

"Sure," Shayne said, slowly backing away. "But Conrad's gone now. And by the time I get Russell out of my house, he probably will have moved on to someone else. And if BJ ever does come up with something, Thomas will have already taken you down. And so what if Fifi did have her baby? Looks like she'll be dead before she has a chance to raise him."

Violet reached out to Shayne, but she backed away with her hands in the air.

"No, Violet, I'm done. Your plan has resulted in nothing short of an all-out catastrophe. So just leave me alone and stay out of my life." And with that, Shayne turned around and ran toward the exit.

Violet wanted to go after her, but she just didn't have the energy. At this point, all she cared about was helping Fifi get well. After that, maybe she'd have it in her to deal with Shayne.

But as she walked back into Fifi's hospital room, Violet couldn't help but replay every word Shayne had just spoken and wonder if, on some level, she was right.

# The Admission

# CHAPTER THIRTY-TWO

Violet sat behind her desk and stared at the computer screen blankly. For the past hour, she'd been persuading herself to write an email that she had decided to send to Shayne, Fifi, BJ, Conrad, and Bodie. But she was having a hard time. She couldn't seem to face what she needed to say.

It had been over a month since Fifi's accident, and she'd refused to leave the house or see anyone. Violet had convinced Bodie, who was completely exhausted from caring for both Fifi and the baby, to let her come over just to say hello and drop off meals that Rita had prepared. But when Violet got there, Fifi barely looked at her, let alone spoke. The only people she allowed near her were Bodie and Lance. And while Bodie swore that Fifi wasn't mad at or blaming her for the accident, Violet begged to differ.

Shayne hadn't spoken to Violet since the day of Fifi's accident. Since then, according to BJ, Shayne had pretty much given up on being with Conrad and convinced herself that she'd be stuck with Russell for the rest of her life. And Conrad, believing that Shayne and Russell were officially back together, had been dealing with the pain of it all by throwing himself into his work at the construction company.

And poor BJ. He was so stressed out that he had to be put on high blood pressure medication. The surveillance cameras and recording devices he'd set up at Thomas' house had yet to reveal a thing. A special passcode had been set up on Thomas' computer system that protected important records BJ was trying to access, including his taxes and financials from deals he'd worked on with elderly real estate developers who could easily be swindled.

Problem was, BJ couldn't seem to get around or figure out

the passcode. As a result, he told Violet he felt guilty for failing her. He also felt responsible for the letter that Thomas had sent her yesterday, stating she had forty-eight hours to sign over her half of the business before he took it and revealed the identity of Britney Ciara's father. Most importantly, BJ was afraid that this entire plan would end unsuccessfully, and he would never reunite with his wife and children.

But in the end, everything that had taken place over the past few months came down to the fault of one person. Violet. So now that everyone involved felt as though her plan had torn their lives apart, she knew it was time to take responsibility, attempt to make amends, and help put their lives back together in whatever way she could.

Violet took a deep breath and placed her trembling fingers onto the keyboard, then began typing.

*Dear Friends,*

*I hope that this email finds you all as well as you can possibly be during this trying time. Let me start by sending a heartfelt apology to each of you for the failure of my plan. As I hope everyone knows, my intentions were ambitious, but good. Shayne, I so wanted to help you find a man who could give you the love that you deserve. Fifi, I wanted to provide you with the protection that you and Lance needed, along with the companionship of someone who would truly appreciate you and the baby.*

*BJ, Conrad, and Bodie, we developed such a strong bond while you were in prison. I wanted nothing more than to see the three of you out in the world, surrounded by caring people, and sharing all of your goodness and talents with those who deserve it.*

*But unfortunately, even the best-laid plans sometimes have a way of going awry. The best intentions can take a turn for the worst. As a result of my plan, we have all experienced our fair share of setbacks. But my hope is that we can resist dwelling on that. I am tired of harboring ill feelings over the actions of others, and I hope that you all are as well.*

*It is not my fault that Elliot got involved with an unscrupulous business partner and impregnated his underage daughter. Shayne, it is not your fault that your husband ended up being a weak, superficial man who turned his back on his family when they needed him the most. Fifi, it is not your fault that the man you thought loved you turned out to be a ruthless bastard who would rather take your life and the life of your child than risk his political career.*

*As for you BJ, Conrad, and Bodie, know that I only wanted to provide the three of you with the lives that you so wanted to live. BJ, I wanted us to triumph over Thomas so that you could go back to your family with your head held high. Conrad, I tried to provide you with the family that you so desired but missed out on after the unexpected death of your girlfriend. And Bodie, after what you went through with your sister, I knew how much you would love to watch over a special, expectant mother.*

*But now that things have not quite gone as planned, I am offering to do whatever I can to assist each of you in rebuilding your lives. If there is anything that you need, please let me know, and I will do everything in my power to make it happen. You all know how to contact me, so please feel free to do so whenever you're ready. And again, I hope you all accept my sincerest apology.*

*With best wishes,*

*Violet*

The minute she went to click the *send* button, her computer crashed. Violet tried repeatedly to turn it back on, but to no avail. She thought of calling BJ, but he was still at Thomas'.

Violet picked up her glass and meandered upstairs, deciding that she'd take a long hot bubble bath while waiting for BJ to come home and get her computer back up and running.

# THE JACKPOT

# CHAPTER THIRTY-THREE

"**B**J!" Violet called out the minute she heard him walk through the door. "My computer crashed! Can you go take a look at it?"

"Vi, get in the library! *Now!*" he yelled.

"What?" Violet asked as she walked down the hallway.

"Get in here." BJ pointed toward the desk, his eyes dancing wildly.

"Before you get started," Violet said, "I need for you to fix my computer. It crashed, and I've got a very important email that I need to —"

"Vi, please sit down." BJ pulled several of the surveillance cameras out of his bag and placed them on the desk.

"What are you doing?" Violet asked, her screeching tone filled with alarm. "Why did you take the cameras out of Thomas' house?"

BJ remained silent as he frantically plopped down behind her desk. He banged away at the computer keyboard for several minutes, rebooted the hard drive, then waited. As soon as the computer came back on, Violet sighed with relief.

"*Thank* you," she said, motioning for BJ to get up. "Now can you please tell me why you —"

"Vi. *Sit.*"

Violet looked at him confusingly while he plugged one of the camera's video receivers into the computer. BJ's face was bright red and drenched with sweat.

"Are you all right?" she asked, walking around to the other side of the desk and sitting down slowly.

"At this very moment," BJ said, clicking the mouse and hitting the keyboard vigorously, "I am better than ever." He looked up at Violet then swung the computer monitor in her direction.

She focused on the screen and saw an elaborately decorated, bright pink bedroom. Britney Ciara was lying in the middle of the floor with her diaper hanging off, crying a river as her arms and legs were flailing about.

Next to the baby was Madison, who was busy pouring small white crystals inside a glass pipe. She lit a fire underneath it, gently placed the pipe inside her mouth and inhaled deeply. As the baby continued to thrash, Madison took several more puffs, then dropped the pipe and sprawled out onto the floor.

Violet covered her mouth and leaned in closer to the screen, watching as Madison's eyes rolled into the back of her head. She could barely breathe while anxiously waiting to see what would happen next. That's when BJ said, "Oh, that scene's gonna last for hours."

Violet shook her head and swallowed hard. "I don't believe this."

"And it doesn't stop there. When I was in Thomas' office this morning, I mentioned going up to Madison's room to install some new games on her computer. But Thomas told me to wait because she was probably still *smoking her breakfast*."

"Nooo!" Violet said, shaking her head in disbelief.

"Yes, he did. And when I asked him what he meant, he said that Madison was probably smoking her first helping of crystal meth of the day."

"So, he knows she's on drugs, and he's not even trying to help her?"

BJ snorted loudly. "*Help* her. He's using it to his advantage! Because get this. When I asked Thomas if Madison was addicted, he said, *Of course. How else do you think I convinced her to let a troll like Elliot impregnate her?*"

"*What*?!" Violet screamed, jolting back so swiftly that she almost fell out of her chair. She held onto the edge of the desk for dear life, salivating at the thought of all the things she'd say to Thomas while he signed his life over to her.

"And the best part is," BJ said, "I got every word of it on tape."

Violet balled her hands into fists and threw her arms in the air, forming a perfect V for victory. But before she could break out into a cheer, BJ continued.

"I'm not done," he said, pulling file after file out of his briefcase. "Remember how we'd always discuss Thomas' ties to the mafia? Well, he's still got 'em, but their much stronger than we ever knew."

Violet opened a file containing stacks of bank records as BJ went on.

"Thomas has been accepting huge amounts of money from several well-known crime bosses and cleaning the funds through the real estate company."

"And you have proof of that in these files?"

"Absolutely. And the tax report file shows that Thomas hasn't been reporting all of his monies earned to the government, either."

"How did you *get* all this?" Violet asked, her eyes widening while she flipped through the papers.

"You know how I couldn't figure out Thomas' computer passcode? Well, I realized that the camera in his office was recording him typing it in. So, I reviewed the footage, got the code, and gained access to everything."

"You're a genius, pure and simple."

"Why thank you," BJ replied proudly. He and Violet stared at one another in triumphant silence for several moments before she finally spoke up.

"Guess what?"

"What?"

"We did it."

"We did, didn't we?"

The twosome jumped up and embraced one another. But as Violet relished in the moment, her heart suddenly sank. Because in spite of the good news she'd just received, she still had an email to send out.

"I'll get it," BJ said, strutting out of the room.

"Get what?"

"The door. Didn't you hear the bell ring?"

"No," Violet said, looking back at the computer screen. The video of Madison's bedroom was still playing, and Madison was still passed out on the floor while Britney Ciara continued to wail next to her.

"She's in the library," Violet heard BJ tell someone a few seconds later.

"Thanks," a female voice replied.

Violet watched the entryway as she heard high heels clicking down the hall. A few seconds later, Shayne's head appeared in the doorway. "Hey. Can I come in?" she asked meekly while struggling to keep her balance.

"Please," Violet said, her tone cool despite the sight of Shayne warming her heart.

She entered the room and sat down next to Violet, staring at her apologetically before grabbing her hand. Shayne's blinking eyes appeared to be struggling to hold back tears. "I'm sorry," she whispered.

"So am I," Violet replied, squeezing her hand.

"I uh . . . I said some things to you that I—"

"Forget about it," Violet said as the guilt of failing her friends fell heavily upon her.

"I have something that I want to show you," Shayne said, "And something I have to tell you."

"Oh . . . okay."

Shayne pulled out her cell phone, her sorrowful expression quickly transforming into one of amusement. "You're not going to believe this."

"Well let's hear it. And see it," Violet said.

"Okay. So last weekend Matthew and his boyfriend Phillip went to a gay club where transvestites perform. During the *Jessica Simpson* impersonator's performance, Matthew said that the singer kept staring at him and seemed to be serenading him. Of course this infuriated Phillip, so when the singer approached Matthew after the show, his boyfriend was ready to pounce. But then the impersonator, who goes by the name Jade, asked Matthew if his father's name is Russell. When Matthew said yes, Jade proceeded to tell Matthew that he'd been having an affair with Russell for the past year—"

"Wait, *what*?" Violet leaned back and stared at Shayne through wide eyes.

"Some male *Jessica Simpson* impersonator told Matthew that he's been having an affair with Russell!" Shayne repeated.

Violet sat motionless and allowed this outrageous information to sink in. When it finally did, she laughed so hard that she almost suffocated. She clutched her throbbing abdomen and motioned for Shayne to continue.

"This impersonator told Matthew that he was the reason Russell left me, and that they were actually living together. Matthew told him that was impossible since he and the kids spent weekends at Russell's apartment. But Jade claimed that he just hid his things and stayed at a hotel whenever they were there."

"How in the hell did Russell meet this Jade?" Violet wheezed, her stomach now in knots.

"At the club where he performs. Russell was there one night for his co-worker's birthday party. And now, according to Matthew, Jade is furious because Russell just up and left him to move back in with us. He said that Russell won't take his calls, and even threatened to kill him if he ever showed up at his home or job. And guess what? *Jade's* the one who's been calling the house constantly and hanging up."

"And I'm sure Russell knew that when he insisted it was Conrad and tried to attack you. He just used that to try and deflect from their affair and guilt you into having sex with him."

"Exactly. So back to Matthew. Of course he didn't believe Jade's claims, which is where this comes in," Shayne said, holding her phone in the air.

"You wouldn't happen to have some sort of salacious video or photos on there, now would you?"

"Why yes, I believe I have both," Shayne said, smiling wickedly.

"*No-o-o.*"

"*Ye-e-es,*" Shayne sang, opening the video file on her phone.

When Russell's image popped up on the screen, Violet screamed and jumped out of her seat. He was standing on the side of a bed, naked and holding the head of a petite young man. The young man, who was also naked, was sitting on the edge of the bed giving Russell a blow job.

"This can't be real," Violet uttered, barely able to breathe while watching the video. She gasped and grabbed Shayne's arm as Russell thrust his hips vigorously and gripped Jade's neck so tightly that his long blond wig fell off.

"Oh, it's real," Shayne said, closing out the file. "I'll spare you the rest."

"Which would entail . . ."

"Anal, back end oral, golden showers—"

"Whoa. That's enough. I get the picture. But wait, how did you get your hands on that video?"

"Jade sent it to Matthew as proof of the affair. And do you know that the reason Russell gave Jade for leaving him was that the kids and I just couldn't get on without him, and that we were all on the verge of nervous breakdowns?"

"Russell has completely lost his mind," Violet said.

"I know. So, it's a good thing I now have all the ammo I need to get him the hell out of my house and Conrad back in . . . that is if he still wants to come back."

"Of course he wants to come back. Do you know how sick he is of living with BJ and me, and how much he misses you?"

"Really? So . . . he's not seeing anybody?"

"Absolutely not! Give yourself a little credit, Shayne. You're not that easy to get over."

"I guess I'm not," Shayne said, grinning wildly. "Is he here?"

"No, he's still at the office. But he'll be back soon. Why don't I have Rita fix us some lunch while we wait for him?"

"That sounds good."

"And I'll have BJ download that video and whatever pictures you have onto my computer so you'll have backups, just in case you need them."

"That would be awesome. I'm sure I'll need a backup after I play this video for Russell when he gets back to the house tonight. He'll probably end up losing his shit and breaking my phone!" Shayne said as they headed to the dining room. On the way there, she turned to Violet. "So . . . do you forgive me for the things I said to you?"

"There's nothing to forgive. You were angry. The man you love was taken away from you and the man you hate forced himself back in. I understood where you were coming from when you said those things."

"I was still wrong."

"You were just speaking your mind."

"But the least I could've done was spoken a little less abrasively."

"Now I won't argue with you there," Violet said before she and Shayne broke out into laughter. Once they quieted down,

Violet turned to Shayne. "Have you spoken to Fifi?"

"Not in a while. I talked to her a few times after the accident, but then she stopped taking my calls. Bodie said she just doesn't want to see or talk to anybody."

"I feel so badly about what happened," Violet said, sitting down at the head of the dining room table and buzzing Rita. "Responsible even."

"Don't," Shayne said firmly, sitting next to her. "That was not your fault. The only person who's responsible for what happened to Fifi is Edward."

Rita's voice interrupted the conversation. "Yes, ma'am?"

"Could you please prepare two lobster and crab salads for lunch?" Violet asked.

"Ooh, I love those," Shayne said.

"I know. That's why I requested them."

"And to drink?" Rita asked.

"The white wine that's chilling in the refrigerator."

"Yes, ma'am."

"So, what should we do about Fifi?" Shayne asked Violet.

"I don't know. She won't talk to me, either. I wish she would let me send her, Bodie, and the baby away so that they'll be safe."

"Me, too. I'm afraid for them. Especially now that Edward is running for president."

"I think we should have Bodie arrange an intervention," Violet said. "We'll go over there whether Fifi wants to see us or not and convince her that she needs to get out of town. I would hate for all of us to have gone into this as a threesome without all three of us coming out of it successfully."

"So, you're still hopeful that something will come of the surveillance system you set up at Thomas'?"

Violet looked at Shayne perplexedly before realizing that she hadn't told her about all that BJ had uncovered.

"Lunch is served, ladies," Rita said, rolling a cart into the room.

"Thank you," Violet replied before telling Shayne, "BJ and I made some serious strides today. I'll give you the short version so that as soon as Conrad gets home, you can go tell him your good news about Russell."

And with that, Shayne dug into her salad while Violet filled her in on everything.

# THE RESURFACING

# CHAPTER THIRTY-FOUR

"To ending the last chapter and beginning the next," Shayne said as she held her champagne glass in the air.

"Hear, hear," Conrad replied, clinking his glass against hers.

Violet glanced over at the two empty seats to her left. "You're proposing the toast a little early, aren't you?"

"Sorry," Shayne responded, lowering her glass and running her hand down her silk emerald green halter dress. "I guess I'm just . . . excited."

Violet was hosting a dinner party for Shayne in celebration of Russell's departure, who had moved out early that morning, and Conrad's return, who had moved back in later that morning. She'd extended an invitation to Fifi and Bodie, but the soiree had begun almost an hour ago, and they had yet to arrive.

"Ma'am?" Rita said softly over the intercom.

"Yes?" Violet responded.

"Would you like for me to serve the hors d' oeuvres now?"

Violet glanced around the table. Her guests looked back at her longingly. She sighed deeply. "Yes, please."

BJ reached over and patted Violet's arm. "You look really beautiful tonight. That *Prada* tux fits you beautifully."

"Nice try," she said, draining her glass as Rita rolled in the hors d' oeuvres.

"So, who wants to hear about what happened when I confronted Russell about his young male lover?" Shayne asked.

"I think I speak for everyone when I say we all do!" Conrad replied.

"Okay!" Shayne said. "So, the afternoon that Matthew

showed me the infamous sex tape, I called Russell at work and asked what time he'd be home. He said about six o' clock. I lowered my voice and whispered for him to meet me in the bedroom when he got there. Of course he took the bait, and he started panting heavily and asking a bunch of raunchy questions, which is when I hung up on him. At six o' clock on the dot, Russell came charging up the stairs and burst through the bedroom door. When he saw me lying in bed with the comforter pulled up to my neck, he broke out into a huge grin, because of course he thought I was nude."

Conrad shook his head and chuckled softly. "As Shayne's kids like to say, he thought it was about to be on and poppin'!"

"Exactly!" Shayne squeezed Conrad's arm affectionately. "So then Russel ripped off his blazer and practically tore the buttons off his shirt as he walked toward the bed. But he stopped dead in his tracks when he heard his own moans coming from my tablet. You should have seen the look of terror in his eyes when he saw himself having anal sex with Jade, without a condom no less. I swear the way Russell gripped his chest and fell to his knees, I thought he was having a heart attack."

BJ covered his face, his shoulders shaking with laughter. "I'm sorry, but that is absolutely hilarious. What did he have to say for himself?"

"You mean what did he wheeze? Because the man could barely talk! He somehow eked out a barely audible, *What . . . is . . . this*. That's when I threw the comforter off and revealed that I was fully dressed, opened the bedroom door, and told Russell to tell *Jessica Simpson* I said hi when he called to tell her he'd be moving back in."

The group gave Shayne a round of applause.

"I love it," Violet said. "I wish you could've recorded that entire moment with Russell —"

179

She stopped abruptly after hearing a commotion outside of the dining room. When Violet looked up, she saw Fifi hobbling into the room on crutches and Bodie following closely behind her.

"Hello everyone," Fifi said quietly, as Bodie pulled a chair out for her.

"Hi," Shayne said. The men nodded their hellos. Then all eyes turned to Violet, who was so moved that Fifi had actually shown up that she couldn't even speak.

"Thanks for having us," Bodie said to Violet before turning to Shayne and Conrad. "Hey, congratulations you two."

"Thank you," Conrad said.

Violet took a deep breath and gathered herself. "I'm so glad you all came. Please, help yourselves to the champagne and hors d' oeuvres. Rita will be serving the main course soon."

"Sounds good," Bodie said, pouring mineral water for Fifi and champagne for himself.

Violet sat down and turned to Fifi. "It's so good to see you."

"You too. But I came to do more than just celebrate Shayne and Conrad's reunion. When dinner is over, Bodie and I would like to speak with you."

"Oh . . . I . . . okay," Violet stammered, picking up her glass and draining it in one gulp. Then she hit the intercom button. "Rita, can you bring in a bottle of *Ketel One* when you serve the main course?"

"Yes, ma'am."

Shayne reached over and grabbed Fifi's hand. "I'm guessing you haven't heard about what happened with Russell."

Fifi shook her head while biting into a glazed pear. "I haven't, and I'm hoping it's nothing tragic. I don't need to hear any bad news right now."

"Oh no honey, you're gonna love this . . ."

As Shayne began rehashing her salacious tale, Violet refilled her glass and contemplated all the things Fifi would probably have to say to her.

"So . . ." Violet said from across her desk, her hands folded tightly in her lap. At Fifi's request, she was meeting with her and Bodie alone in the library. "What can I do for you two?"

Fifi took a deep breath and looked over at Bodie, who wrapped his arm around her. She dabbed the corners of her eyes then turned to Violet. "Bodie and I have decided to . . . um . . ." When her voice trailed off, Bodie spoke up.

"We were thinking that maybe it's time for us to move forward with your protection program idea."

Violet sat back and let out a huge sigh, realizing that she'd been holding her breath practically since she'd sat down. "Are you sure?"

Fifi reached over and squeezed Bodie's hand. "Yes. We've been talking about it for a while now, because we just don't feel safe ever since . . . you know."

"And even though we really want to stay in Fifi's parents' house and raise Lance in this neighborhood, we think it would be best to just cut out."

Violet's expression melted into utter sadness at the thought of her friends moving away. "I hate that it's come to this, but you all are doing the right thing. I've been so afraid for you both, but I've been terrified ever since the—"

"So where do we start?" Fifi asked, interrupting Violet before she could finish her statement.

Violet caught the hint and got right down to business. "I think we should begin by doing name changes, then creating passports, choosing a location out of the country where you'd both feel comfortable—" She stopped abruptly when a stream of tears began pouring down Fifi's face. "I'm so sorry," she whispered.

"No, it's okay," Fifi told her, sniffling while Bodie held her tightly. "Go ahead."

Violet stood up. "I'll tell you what. Why don't you let me get started on everything, and then we can meet again when I've made some progress. We don't have to do this now." She walked around the desk and helped Fifi out of her chair. "Go on home and get some rest. I'll call you in a couple of days and let you know where I'm at with things."

"That sounds like a plan," Bodie said, grabbing Fifi's crutches and handing them to her. "We really appreciate this, Vi."

Violet led the pair out of the room and showed them to the door. "It's the least I can do. You all be careful. And thanks again for coming. I've really missed you both."

"You, too," Fifi said, leaning in and kissing her on the cheek. "Talk to you soon."

Violet watched Fifi and Bodie until they made it into their house safely. Then she called BJ into the library so that he could help her begin working on their relocation.

# THE REDEMPTION

# CHAPTER THIRTY-FIVE

"Hello, Thomas," Violet said coolly as she strolled through his downtown office door.

He jumped up from behind his desk and approached her with open arms. "Violet! It's so good to see you."

Violet held out her hand in order to avoid his embrace. Thomas' employees, who'd immediately began buzzing about frantically when Violet strutted inside the lobby, were walking past his office slowly and peering inside curiously. After Violet called him earlier that week requesting a meeting, she assumed he'd told everyone that the firm was about to be all his.

"Please, have a seat," Thomas said, pulling out a chair.

Violet smoothed the skirt of her tweed cream *Chanel* suit and sat down gingerly. When Thomas plopped down across from her, she smiled pleasantly and placed her briefcase on the desk.

"It's good to know you finally came to your senses," he said. "I would've hated to have put you through the humiliation of everyone finding out about Elliot and Madison's little tryst, not to mention Britney Ciara. And you cut it pretty close, too. One more day and the cat would've been outta the bag."

"Lucky me," Violet replied, opening the briefcase and removing her laptop.

"Well, let's get to it then." Thomas opened a drawer and removed a file folder. "I've got everything that you need to sign right here. My lawyers reviewed the paperwork, and everything's in order. So once your John Hancock's in place, we'll be set, and you will finally be rid of me."

Violet opened a video file on her computer titled *Evidence*.

"Yeah, about that. What do you say we switch gears, and you sign your half of the company over to me instead?"

Thomas laughed wildly, his oversized neon white veneers on full display. "*Excuse* me? Now, why would I do that?"

"Because I've got some shit on you that equates Elliot impregnating your daughter to elementary school fodder."

"Oh, really? Violet, you weak, stupid, plastic, superficial excuse for a woman, what could you possibly have on me?"

"Take a look," Violet replied icily, tapping a button on her computer and turning it toward Thomas so that he could see the image of Madison doing drugs and Britney Ciara crying hysterically right next to her. As Thomas' face fell in horror, Violet pulled several files out of her briefcase. "And that's not all. Cheating Uncle Sam, laundering money for the mob, getting your daughter hooked on crystal meth and encouraging her affair with my husband. Shall I continue?"

Thomas grunted and waved his hand at the laptop. "Shut that thing off. How in the hell did you even get that footage?"

"That's none of your concern." Violet spread several papers across the desk. "So, what's it gonna be? Would you like to sign your half of this company over to me and pay out all the money you owe? Or shall I release—"

"Just give me the goddamn papers, you spiteful bitch."

"Now, now, Thomas. You're already going to rot in hell. Why don't you watch your language before God punishes you severely while you're still here on earth?"

"I should have taken you out when I had the chance," Thomas muttered as he pushed his toupee back, which kept sliding forward thanks to his sweaty scalp.

"Oh, wait, I forgot! There's also footage of your sweet little daughter Madison giving head to three different guys simultaneously, right in front of the baby no less. Would you like to—"

"Get the fuck out of here," Thomas spewed, shoving the

papers back at her after signing them. "I'll have my accountant messenger over a check this afternoon, you fucking . . ." he grumbled under his breath.

Violet shut down the computer and put it along with her files back inside her briefcase.

"Do you know what the best part of all this is?" she asked cheerily before standing up and heading toward the door. "I'm *still* not done with you yet."

"What else could you possibly do?"

"I'll be in touch . . ."

Violet glided out the door. When she saw everyone gathered in the lobby, she stopped and displayed her best beauty pageant smile.

"I'll see you all first thing Monday morning," she told them, watching as they stared back at her in confusion. "I'm sure Thomas will come out and explain everything to you shortly. Good day."

And with that, she floated out the door, grabbed her cell phone and called BJ to tell him to start packing.

# CHAPTER THIRTY-SIX

"Is that everything?" Fifi asked Bodie as she searched through the kitchen cabinets.

"That's everything," Bodie replied, looking around at the stacks of boxes surrounding them.

"I still can't believe it's come to this," she said quietly. "I'm letting this man drive me not only out of my house, but out of the country."

"Do you have any other choice?"

"I guess not." Fifi looked down at Lance as he slept peacefully. "He's certainly worth it. But if someone would've told me that my life was going to come to this, I would have never believed them."

Bodie peered down at the baby. "Well, sometimes the choices we make lead us in directions that we never thought we'd go. Luckily you got something beautiful out of the deal."

"I did. And I'm so glad you're coming with us. You know you can still back out of this if you want."

"Why would I do that? Where else do I have to go? You and Lance are my family now. Wherever you all are is where I wanna be."

"Thank you," Fifi whispered.

"I guess I'd better start loading up the truck." Bodie grabbed a few boxes right before the phone rang. "You got it?"

"Yep, I got it." Fifi reached over and grabbed her cell. "Hello?"

"He's dead."

"What?"

"He's dead."

"Who is this?" Fifi asked.

"Carol. Edward's wife."

Fifi almost dropped the phone. She swallowed hard, then cleared her throat. "H-how can I help you?"

"I'm calling to tell you that Edward is dead."

"I'm sorry. Edward's *what*?"

"Dead. I would've come to your home to tell you personally, but I just . . ."

"Wait. I'm sorry. I just . . ." Fifi closed her eyes and sat back. "He's dead. As in deceased. Flatlined. Is that what you're saying?"

"Yes. That's what I'm saying."

Fifi jumped up from the couch and began pacing the floor, a surge of adrenaline shooting throughout her body. "*How*? What happened?"

"I killed him."

"You . . . you killed him?" Fifi asked, falling back down onto the couch, as she suddenly felt faint.

"Yes. I killed him."

"Why?"

"It was self-defense."

"He tried to hurt you?"

"Yes," Carol murmured.

"But why would he do that?"

"Because I overheard him talking to a hit man. About you."

Fifi's breath caught in her throat as her stomach rumbled ferociously. "And . . . and what did he say?"

"That he . . . that he had your parents killed."

"*Nooo*," Fifi sobbed.

"Yes. He did. I heard him tell the hitman that he should have blown your house up just like he did your parents' instead of trying to run you and the baby over."

Fifi fell forward. She moaned loudly and hugged her knees tightly. Bodie walked back inside and started to grab another stack of boxes until he saw her doubled over.

"What's wrong?" he asked, rushing to her side. "Who are you talking to?"

"Edward's wife," she whispered before turning her attention back to the call. "I'm confused, Carol. The chief said that the fire at my parents' house was caused by an electrical problem."

"Edward paid him to say that."

"Oh God," Fifi moaned before Carol continued.

"After I received your initial letter stating that you were pregnant by Edward, he insisted that you were some crazy stalker he'd only met at a rally. Then when I received your last letter stating you had lied about the pregnancy, I took both you and Edward at your word and assumed that was the end of it. So you can imagine how I felt when I overheard Edward's conversation."

"Carol, I wanted you to know the truth. And I hope you understand I had no idea Edward was married when we met. By the time I found out, it was too late."

"Well, the baby's here now. And he deserves to be here, which is why I was so shocked when I overheard how determined Edward was to have you both killed."

"Thank you. I really appreciate that . . ." Fifi hesitated, but when curiosity overcame her, she blurted out, "So how did you kill him?"

"*What?*" Bodie yelled.

Fifi pressed her finger against her lips and nodded her head as Carol continued.

"I stormed into the room, snatched the phone out of Edward's hand and slammed it down onto the floor. Then I slapped him and asked how he could've brought a child into the world without telling me, had someone kill your parents, then attempt to kill you and the baby." Her voice grew shaky, and she paused.

"Go ahead," Fifi said softly. "It's okay."

"So . . . so once Edward got over the fact that I'd heard his conversation and confronted him in the manner that I had, he pushed me down onto the floor. He glared at me with this evil look on his face and told me to stay out of his affairs, then picked the phone back up and continued speaking with his campaign manager. I got up and tried to take the phone away from him again, and he punched me in the eye with it."

"Oh no," Fifi gasped.

"Edward kept hitting me in the face until I fell to the floor. When he thought I'd passed out, he went back to his call. That's when I crept into the drawer, pulled out his gun, and shot him. When the authorities got there and saw my face then heard my story, they didn't even question me."

"Carol, I'm so sorry you went through all that."

"And I'm sorry you went through all that you did as well. I want you to know that I'm going to set up a trust fund for the baby, too."

"That's really generous of you. Thank you." Fifi glanced over at Bodie, who was staring at her with an alarmed expression on his face. She reached over and placed her hand on his leg, then continued her conversation. "Carol, did you mention what happened to me and my parents to the authorities?"

"No, I didn't. I wanted to talk to you first. But if you want me to report it, I'd be more than happy—"

"Absolutely not," Fifi told her. "We've both been through enough. I know the truth, you know the truth, and that's really all that matters. Plus, Edward's no longer here, so as far as I'm concerned, justice has already been served."

"I agree."

Fifi felt as if one hundred pounds of stress had been lifted from her shoulders. "Carol, thank you for calling and sharing all this with me. And for being so understanding about the baby."

"You're welcome. Maybe one day I can meet . . ."

"Lance. I named him after my father."

"How lovely. I would love to meet him at some point. But not anytime soon. I don't think I have it in me right now after all that's happened."

"Of course. I completely understand. Just know that my door is always open."

"Thank you. And I'll let you know once the trust fund has been set up."

"I appreciate that, Carol. Take care of yourself."

"You too, Fifi. Goodbye."

Fifi hung up the phone and threw her arms around Bodie. "Unpack the boxes. We're staying here!"

"So wait, Edward's wife *killed* him? What the hell happened?"

Fifi reached down and grabbed her phone. "Hold on, I need to call Violet and let her know we're not leaving. You can listen in while I tell her the story."

"Hello?" Fifi heard Violet say in the midst of screaming in the background.

"Hey! What's going on over there?"

"That's Shayne," Violet shouted. "Conrad just proposed to her."

"Oh, my goodness! That's wonderful. But I've got news that's gonna top that."

"Could it top the fact that Thomas signed his half of the company over to me today and paid back all the money he owed?"

"I believe so."

"Well, let's hear it then."

"Edward's dead! His wife just called to tell me that she killed him!"

Violet fell silent. All Fifi could hear was Shayne shouting in the background.

"Did you hear what I just said?" Fifi asked her.

"I couldn't have possibly heard you correctly. Could you please repeat that?"

"I'll do you one better. We'll come over so that I can repeat myself in person."

"Please do," Violet said.

"See you in a minute."

As soon as Fifi hung up the phone, Bodie picked her up and swung her around.

"We're free!" she said before kissing him square in the mouth.

Bodie was so surprised he almost dropped her. But he had no time to recover as Fifi took his head in her hands and kissed him deeply. After several moments, she pulled away and whispered, "I love you."

"I love you, too." Bodie leaned in and initiated another kiss, then carried her to the bedroom.

"Violet's expecting us," she said in between kisses.

"I've been waiting for this moment for months. Violet can wait an hour or so."

And with that, Bodie gently laid Fifi down and proceeded to make slow, passionate love to her.

# The Pretense II

# CHAPTER THIRTY-SEVEN

Violet Christianson's name alone now meant more than it ever had before to those around her. All who knew Violet no longer just wanted her, wanted to be her, or simply wanted her to go away. Now everyone actually wanted to be down with Violet. Be on her team. Be an intricate part of her exclusive entourage.

While Violet was still extraordinarily beautiful, no one seemed to care about her looks anymore — because everyone was too busy focusing on her accomplishments. For Violet was doing big things these days, the most noticeable being that she had practically taken over the real estate industry.

It no longer mattered that Violet once had the richest husband on the block. Because she was now considered the richest woman in the state. And it wasn't because she was married to money. It was because she was making it on her own.

It also no longer mattered that Violet still lived in the biggest house on the block. Because she was now selling houses ten times the size of hers. And while she could have easily afforded to move into any home she wanted, Violet was happy and comfortable right where she was. Because her house and her block that her best friends still lived on had been good to her.

Violet Christianson. Important, admired, and able to make the impossible possible. All the reasons why everyone wanted to be down with her, be on her team, and be an intricate part of her exclusive entourage.

# CHAPTER THIRTY-EIGHT

Shayne Wentworth was not only still considered the sweetest woman on the block, but she was now considered the luckiest.

People no longer saw Shayne as the ex-beauty pageant queen who was carrying a few extra pounds. She was now the voluptuous bombshell whose green eyes were dancing, clear skin was glowing, and blonde locks were shining more than ever before. Shayne was no longer considered just a mere post-pageant contender, but a grand prize winner who had rid herself of one husband in order to acquire a better one.

Shayne's new husband Conrad might not have been the most powerful man on the block as Russell once had, but he certainly was the most desirable. And while Russell was once viewed as a good father, Conrad had stepped up and become a great one, helping to totally turn Shayne's household around. Plus, his good paying job at Violet's company still allowed Shayne to stay at home while he provided for the family. So the lifestyle Shayne had grown accustomed to not only remained the same, but improved quite considerably.

And while Shayne's house was still bursting with activity, it was now all positive. Her children were doing wonderfully, and they'd handled the fact that their father was going to jail well. A couple of them even seemed happy. Shayne certainly was. But she'd tried her best to hide it.

Shayne Wentworth. Sexy, confident, and stronger than she'd ever been before. Thanks to her overall glow up and renewed family life, she had actually become the most envied woman on the block.

# Chapter Thirty-nine

Fifi Gentry was not only still considered the feistiest woman on the block, but she was also considered the strongest.

Everyone knew that some crazed individual who was probably upset over some bill that Fifi helped to get passed had tried to hurt her. But they saw how quickly she'd dusted herself off and kept it moving. People admired her determination and tenacity to continue standing up for what she believed in, even if it meant risking her life.

And while Fifi was still the only woman on the block who had never been married, at least she was engaged. Bodie proposed to her the day after they found out about Edward's death. He admitted that he'd fallen in love with her the minute he climbed inside the limo when they picked him up from jail. And while Fifi confessed that she couldn't echo those same sentiments, she did admit to Bodie that he'd grown on her over time.

Nine months ago, Fifi's house wasn't bursting with any sort of activity, but it certainly was now. She'd always dreamed of raising a family in the same house that she had grown up in, but now she was doing it with a man she loved. And while Bodie was in the process of adopting Lance, they were already making plans for a second child.

Fifi Gentry. Complete, invincible, and a true survivor. She might have once felt as though she didn't have much, but now she had it all.

# THE TRUTH II

# Chapter Forty

Violet Christianson did indeed appear to have a perfect life. But now, even to herself, she truly did. She had finally been blessed with the one thing that had been missing in her life. A child.

After the check that Thomas had written to her cleared, Violet called to inform him of the final aspect of their deal. In order for her to keep the incriminating evidence she'd gathered under wraps, he would have to allow her to adopt Britney Ciara. At first, both Thomas and Madison put up quite a fuss. But when Violet emailed the incriminating footage that she had of Madison to them both, they proceeded to sign the adoption papers immediately.

But Violet knew none of this would have been possible without her partner in crime, BJ. The minute they'd met in prison, she felt as if he was her spiritual soul mate. It didn't take long to figure out why, after discovering how much they had in common.

BJ realized that he knew Thomas, who Violet had been skeptical of for years. Come to find out, Thomas was the one who'd had BJ's parents killed many years before. Back when his father was running a cleaning business, Thomas would come by his shop and attempt to strong-arm him into paying a weekly fee in exchange for his protection. But BJ's father refused, which was what led to his and his wife's murders.

The family that lived across the street from BJ, who happened to be enemies of Thomas and his cohorts, caught wind of who'd killed BJ's parents. But rather than put hits out and cause an all-out war, they took BJ in and raised him as one of their own. However, BJ kept a promise to both himself and his deceased parents to one day get back at Thomas.

When Violet asked him to be a part of her plan, he had pounced on the opportunity.

Now that BJ's work was done and Violet was all set, he moved to an undisclosed city in Japan where his family had been living under an assumed identity. Violet connected him with a real estate client of hers who owned a computer consulting firm there, and his wife was teaching English at an elementary school. Most importantly, if Thomas ever caught wind of exactly how Violet had obtained all of that damning information, it would be practically impossible for him to find BJ.

Violet Christianson. Slick, loyal, and bad to the bone. If everyone knew the truth about her, she would never be crossed again.

# CHAPTER FORTY-ONE

Shayne Wentworth did indeed appear to have rid herself of one husband in order to acquire a better one. Little did everyone know that her first husband was a raging homosexual who'd left his family because he couldn't handle them, then came running back after she'd met someone else and gotten everything under control.

As for Russell's jail sentence, everyone was under the impression that he had been set up by one of his colleagues who'd accused him of trying to bribe a judge. God forbid they find out that he'd really been arrested for cohabitating and having sexual relations with a minor. Because Jade the *Jessica Simpson* impersonator was only sixteen years old.

As for her new husband, God forbid anyone find out Shayne had gotten him from the clinker. While she knew that he'd been arrested for identity theft, she never asked exactly what he'd done and why, because she honestly didn't care. Shayne was in love, and she knew that Conrad was a good man who'd been rehabilitated. Unfortunately, most people weren't as understanding as she was. And the last thing she wanted to be known as was a convict magnet. So she was willing to work to keep Conrad's past under wraps.

Shayne Wentworth. Still sweet, still reputable, and struggling to keep her secrets buried in order to maintain her reputation. Luckily those around her were too shallow to dig deep enough and unearth her dirt.

# CHAPTER FORTY-TWO

Fifi Gentry had indeed appeared skeptical at the idea of Violet's plan, especially after she found out that Violet wanted to hook her up with a convicted killer. But looks can be deceiving, and underneath it all, Fifi was ecstatic that Violet was assigning her a cold-blooded killer. Because she knew that she could probably talk him into killing Edward.

Fifi was no fool. She only presented herself to be one when it came to Edward. She knew all along that he'd killed her parents. But she played crazy so that when he came up dead, she'd be the last one people suspected. Fifi had already begun the process of interviewing professional hit men who would take Edward out when Violet approached her with the plan. Fifi halted the interviewing process immediately, knowing that she would go through with Violet's idea. But she had to resist the plan for a while because it was all a part of her game. She did it for the effect—because she had to appear as righteous and upstanding as possible.

But Fifi wasn't stupid. And neither was Violet. Which was why Violet hooked her up with a convicted murderer in the first place. Fifi's appreciativeness toward her choice was an unspoken one. But she figured Violet could see it in her eyes. Which was why Violet never let up and waited for her and Shayne to say yes before meeting with the warden.

When Fifi and Bodie decided to change their identities and move away, you'd best believe that they were planning to take Edward out right before they hit the road. And once they were gone, Fifi and Bodie knew that they'd never get caught and would be able to live in anonymous peace.

But then the miracle of Edward's wife killing him occurred. So not only would Fifi and her family be able to stay put, but she wouldn't have a murder and the possibility of getting caught hanging over her head.

Fifi Gentry. Smarter, harsher, and grittier than anyone could have ever imagined. She would've loved to tell everyone just how wrong they'd had her pegged, but like Violet always said, the less they knew, the better.

# YOU MAY ALSO ENJOY THE FOLLOWING FROM EXTASY BOOKS INC:

Shadow of a Man
Denise N. Wheatley

Excerpt

Veronica Level opened her eyes and blinked rapidly. She struggled to clear her blurred vision as she slowly came to. When she was finally able to focus, she gasped at the horrifying scene in front of her.

The smoldering air was filled with thick gray smoke. Cars were piled on top of one another all along the expressway. Horns were blowing, sirens were blaring. Terrified people were jumping out of their burning vehicles, running and screaming. The crowded, five-lane highway had suddenly turned into an apocalyptic warzone.

Veronica gripped her steering wheel and turned around, afraid of what lay behind her. Just as she'd thought, there was more mayhem. Dark clouds loomed overhead. Dozens more overturned cars littered the street, many of them engulfed in flames. She carefully reached for her door handle, hoping that she hadn't broken any bones. Despite feeling shaken and drained, Veronica felt no pain.

She opened the door and stepped outside, bracing herself for the damage that her own car must have sustained. But as Veronica eyed her driver's side, she saw that there was none. Shocked, she rushed around to the passenger side. It too was unscathed. She looked up and saw a bloody man limping toward her, his face distorted in agony as he struggled to support what looked to be a broken right arm.

"You all right?" he heaved.

"Yes, I think so . . . Are you okay?"

"I will be, but I don't know about my wife. She's unconscious. I'm trying to flag down a paramedic." The man looked over at Veronica's car. "There's no damage," he uttered in disbelief. "How in the hell did you manage that?"

"I uh . . . I have no idea . . ."

Veronica turned her head to hide any hint of deceit glimmering in her pale green eyes. She did in fact have an idea as to why her car hadn't been damaged. But she certainly couldn't share that information with a total stranger. Or anyone else for that matter.

Unbelievable . . . Veronica heard the man thinking to himself. How the hell is this woman and her car in pristine condition when the rest of us are out here practically dying? It's unreal. This isn't fair.

Veronica stared at the stranger sympathetically. It was happening again. Just as it always had during intense moments of danger such as this.

The man began looking around frantically as his breathing quickened. Where's the help? he asked himself. We need help! What if Susan dies? And the kids. How will I explain all this to the kids?

"Your wife is going to be fine," Veronica divulged abruptly. "So you won't have to tell your children a thing. Trust me, she'll be fine."

The man stared at Veronica. "Wait, but how did you know that I was even—"

"Is everyone all right over here?" a paramedic asked as he rushed toward them with a medic kit in hand. "Do either of you need assistance?"

"I do!" the man exclaimed, forgetting about Veronica and her cryptic premonition. "My wife, she's still in the car, and I don't know if she's . . ." The man's voice broke.

"Just show me the way, sir," the paramedic said, helping the man walk back to his car. "I'll do whatever I can to save her."

Veronica felt for him and his family. She watched as he limped away, still hearing thoughts of worry flying through his head. Her ability to read minds was still just as powerful as it had ever been. It was a skill that she'd possessed since early childhood. And while she had never really been fascinated by her telepathic ability, it was a phenomenon that her aunt Samantha considered to be a great gift, while her mother, Amanda, had deemed it a freakish curse.

Aunt Samantha always thought of herself as a clairvoyant of sorts, as did Samantha's mother, her mother's mother, and on back through the generations. Samantha's sister Amanda, however, tried to break the chain early on and refused to tap into any sort of psychic abilities that she may have possessed. The last thing Amanda wanted was to be deemed a weirdo by her peers, unlike Samantha, who relished in her telepathy despite being ostracized by their classmates.

During high school, Amanda couldn't help but be embarrassed by Samantha's tendency to accentuate her round baby-face and sinewy figure with dramatically colorful makeup, teased, fiery red hair and flamboyant, gypsy-like clothing. As a result, Amanda felt compelled to downplay her flowing blond locks and pretty, delicate features with simple chignons and modest, classic makeup and attire. The last thing she wanted was to draw even more unwanted attention to the family.

Through the years, Samantha always felt as though her niece, Veronica, possessed a sixth sense that enabled her to see, hear and feel things beyond the average person's capabilities. So the day she discovered that Veronica actually did have the ability to read minds, she was absolutely elated.

It happened one chilly fall evening when Veronica was in the second grade. Samantha had taken her to the local grocery store to pick up last minute Halloween candy. Even though

Amanda insisted that they had enough candy and should've gone out earlier while it was still daylight, Samantha dismissed her, saying that she was overreacting as usual.

Samantha and Veronica went to the market against Amanda's wishes and headed straight to the candy aisle, stocking up on several bags of chocolates and fruity treats. They checked out and walked back through the parking lot toward Samantha's car. On the way there, Veronica noticed two big, burly men dressed in all black, lurking in the back of the lot.

Veronica stopped in her tracks. "Auntie Samantha, look!" she pointed, her finger trembling as her eyes widened.

"Come on, Vee, let's go!" Samantha insisted, grabbing Veronica's little hand out of the air and pulling her along. "If we don't hurry up and get back we'll miss the trick-or-treaters!"

Veronica stumbled behind Samantha reluctantly, scowling at the men in the distance.

This is gonna be easy, she heard one of the men say. But when she looked out at him, he was too far away for her to see his face, let alone hear his voice. All's I gotta do is stick to the plan. I'm grabbin' the kid, Carlos is grabbin' the old bitch, we throw them both in the van then speed off. No sweat.

Veronica squinted, watching fearfully as the men began to walk toward them. Their jumbled thoughts continued to buzz around in her head. Suddenly, it dawned on her that she wasn't hearing the men's voices through her ears. She was hearing their thoughts through her mind.

Veronica stopped again and squeezed Samantha's hand urgently. "They're gonna get us," she whispered.

Samantha stopped and frowned at Veronica. "What are you saying, child?"

"If we go to the car, those men are going get us."

"Look sweetheart, Auntie is in a hurry. Not only do we need to get back for the trick-or-treaters, but my favorite true-crime show comes on in a few minutes. If I miss one second of it, I'm going to be very upset with you."

"Auntie Samantha, I heard them. They said they're gonna throw us in the van and take us!"

Samantha looked at Veronica in dismay and sighed. "Those men?" she pointed, "All the way over there? Honey, how could you even . . ."

# About the Author

Denise N. Wheatley is a lover of romance, happy endings, and the art of storytelling. She strives to create characters who are strong, colorful, and relatable, and tell entertaining stories that embody matters of the heart. She received a B.A. in English from the University of Illinois at Chicago, the city where she was born and raised. When Denise is not sitting behind a computer, you can find her in a movie theater, on a tennis court, watching true crime television or chatting on social media.